warp

Lev Grossman

St. Martin's Griffin
New York

warp

This novel is a work of fiction. All of the events, characters, names, and places depicted in this novel are entirely fictitious or are used fictitiously. No representation that any statement made in this novel is true or that any incident depicted in this novel actually occurred is intended or should be inferred by the reader.

Design by Maureen Troy

Library of Congress Cataloging-in-Publication Data

Grossman, Lev.
    Warp : a novel / Lev Grossman.—1st ed.
       p.   cm.
    ISBN 0-312-17059-9 (trade pbk.)
    I. Title.
    PS3557.R6725W37   1997
    813'. 54—dc21   97-21423
                                                    CIP

First Edition: November 1997

10 9 8 7 6 5 4 3 2 1

For H.

"I'm trying to think who the girl reminds me of," said Hollis.

"Somebody famous."

It was a brilliant, freezing fall day, and the sky was a bright clear blue. Hollis kept his hands in the pockets of his green overcoat. It had a fake fur collar, and all the buttons had fallen off the front.

"Jennifer Holquist, maybe," said Brian.

"Who the hell is that?"

"She was in that TV show. The one about the tennis prodigy."

Hollis squinted into the sun, which was starting to set.

"Did you watch that?" he said. "I can't believe you watched that."

From the top of the hill they looked down at the rest of the park, a huge, empty green field that sloped down and away. In a neat little baseball diamond at the far end, a man and a woman were playing catch with a tennis ball. While they watched he threw her a tricky grounder, which she snapped up one-handed.

"How come you're still here, anyway? Somebody told me you were already gone."

"I am," Brian said. He grinned and started jogging in place to stay warm. "I'm going. I'm fucking history. I'm dust."

"Where are you going?"

"Germany. I have an internship there, in Stuttgart. With Lufthansa. They're putting together some kind of international commission. Airline deregulation. EC stuff. It's a big fat Euro-party."

"What are you going to do for them?"

"I don't really know," said Brian. "It's no big prize — somebody saw my thesis title and jumped on it. I'll just be some kind of glorified gopher, probably."

He held up his hands in protest.

"I'm no hero. Please, ma'am — don't thank me. I'm not a celebrity." Brian was tall and athletic, slightly over six feet, with longish blond hair and a stubbly chin. He was wearing sweats and a blue windbreaker.

Hollis cupped his hands and blew into them to keep warm. The evergreen bushes dotting the park cast long, black shadows back towards them, away from the sun. The wind was making cat's-paws on the coarse green grass.

"Don't take any wooden nickels," said Hollis absently.

He found a thread on the front of his coat and snapped it off.

"How's your German?" he said.

"Bad. You know any?"

"*Kenne nur Bahnhof.*"

"Damn Jerries. Who won the war, anyway?" Brian sniffed and cleared his throat. "And what's with these German girls? They're all like, sophisticated or something. You know who they remind me of? Tasha Yar. You remember that woman on *Star Trek* — the new one? Blond. Slim. Butch, but vulnerable at the same time. Kind of a feminine butchiness. She was the security officer before Worf — she quit after the first year."

"Didn't she get killed?" said Hollis.

"Yeah," said Brian. "That's right. She was eaten by Armus. Armus, the Skin of Evil. Then her acting career started not working out, and she tried to get back on the show. It was complicated — I can't remember it all. She ended up sleeping with a Romulan. It was very complex."

"I should get so lucky," said Hollis.

"It was too much, really." Brian yawned, holding the back of his hand against his teeth. "It's kind of sad. Sometimes I wonder how she's doing. I saw her in a guest spot on some one-season, no-count action series or other. *Dark Justice, Dark Knight, Night Justice* — something like that. She looked depressed. She's even already posed for *Playboy.*"

Hollis hugged himself. All he had on under the overcoat was a cheap black T-shirt with a white Atari logo on it. The plastic stuff of the decal was cracking and flaking like the surface of an old oil painting.

"I'm sure she'll be fine," he said. "She's Frank Sinatra's granddaughter or something."

"Bing Crosby. Jesus Christ, that's her name, for God's sake — Denise Crosby. That actress. She's Bing Crosby's granddaughter."

Across the park was a stretch of road that ran along the edge of the green for a few hundred yards. A white Toyota Camry pulled off it and onto the wide shoulder, crackling across the gravel. It stopped where a few other cars were parked.

"Hell," said Hollis.

"What is it?"

"I knew this would happen."

Hollis walked over a few steps, casually, so that Brian stood between him and the car.

"Jesus, what is this, Hollis?"

"Relax. Just act natural." He crouched down a little. "It's nothing — I'll tell you in a second."

"You know, I really don't have the time to get stuck in the middle of something."

"Who's asking you to? Jesus, just stand still for a second. Just act natural. Be yourself."

The front door of the car opened, and a fit-looking older man with salt-and-pepper gray hair and a mustache got out. He whipped off his hunter-orange baseball cap and shaded his eyes, scanning the park, hands on hips.

"Look at him," said Hollis. "Ever the fashionable little carnivore. God, I have to get out of this city."

The man grimaced, spat on the grass, and sat back down into the car.

At the same time the back door opened and a young black woman in a nylon ski parka got out, tenderly cradling something in her arms. She bumped the door shut with her hip and set the thing gently down on the grass. Immediately it started to scamper off on the end of a leash, and she followed along after it without much enthusiasm.

"That's a ferret," Hollis said. "She does this every day. Same time, same station. I don't even think it likes it all that much—I think ferrets are supposed to live on prairies or something."

Hollis and Brian saw and heard the solid metal *pop* of the trunk opening. The man got back up out of the front seat again, circled around to the rear, and heaved out a bag of golf clubs. Then he locked all the doors with a remote control, slammed shut the trunk, and walked briskly off through a stand of trees and out of sight, the bag of clubs bumping vigorously against his hip.

Hollis straightened up again.

"Who was that?"

"My landlord," said Hollis. "Looks like he's taking a little driving practice. I told him I was going to Aruba for six weeks — if he saw me here there'd be some fireworks, let me tell you."

He kicked at the grass. The pale orange sunlight seemed not to carry any heat, and a cold wind was starting to come up. An empty plastic shopping bag tumbled by, weightless, ten feet over their heads.

"Oh," said Brian. "I saw Eileen Cavanaugh a couple of days ago." He hooked his thumbs into the waistband of his sweat pants. "On the street. I didn't talk to her—I was in a car. She looked different, though. Her hair's all wavy now."

"They always get prettier after we break up," said Hollis. "I hear she has a real-live adult job now—she works at an investment firm downtown, one of those big-time, old-money ones."

"Oh, yeah?" Brian tossed back his blond hair. "Which one?"

In the distance they could hear the high-pitched warning beep of a big truck backing up.

"I don't remember the name."

The air smelled like wet grass. Hollis turned all the way around, slowly, his hands in the pockets of his overcoat, just looking out at the view. By now the road on the other side was completely in the shadow of the little hill they were standing on.

He turned back around to face the sunset again. Looking down at the rolling, sea-green expanse of the park, he was overcome by a rush of memory — something he'd been assigned to read, a long time ago, when he was in elementary school. It was a story.

It was about the ocean.

Tonga lived with his family in a little village by the sea. When Tonga was a little boy, his father made a rule:

"Never, never fish alone at night," he said. "Bring your brother Oba with you. Or better still, do not go at all."

But the summer Tonga turned eleven years old the fishing was very bad, and his family had nothing to eat. His mother fell sick. At last he could wait no longer. One night Tonga stayed awake until his parents were asleep, then he slipped out the window and down to the docks where the fishing boats were kept.

Hollis blinked his eyes against the cold, dry wind.

"So what was she doing?" he said.

"Who? Eileen? Just standing there, I guess. On the sidewalk. Looked like she was having some kind of a sneezing fit."

"She's allergic to practically everything."

"What about this place where she works?" said Brian. "It's in Boston?"

"Sure."

"You don't know where?"

Hollis gestured vaguely.

"It's downtown somewhere. Where all those places are. The financial district, I guess. Jesus, it's not like I memorized the address."

"So you guys don't hang out anymore?" said Brian.

"Not really." Hollis sniffed.

"Maybe I'll give her a call."

"Look, go right ahead. It's a free Commonwealth."

"Say no more — I hear you." Brian held up his hands defensively. "Danger, Will Robinson! Danger!"

He bent over and started stretching his calves. A seagull landed a few yards away, hunting for trash in the tall grass. Down below in the park the woman and the ferret orbited around each other at opposite ends of the leash. The couple had stopped playing catch. They were sitting together on a dugout bench next to the chain-link backstop, drinking cans of soda.

"Jesus, how can they stand that stuff?"

"I didn't even know they had Diet Mountain Dew," said Hollis.

An hour went by, and Tonga still hadn't caught anything. He paddled farther out toward the mouth of the bay, where the water was deepest. Standing up in his skiff, he looped the rope around his wrist and threw out the net one last time.

For a moment nothing happened. Then there was a gentle tug on the line. Tonga looked over the side, down into the water.

A big shape was moving under him, and he heard a little splash, very tiny, and something heaved hard on the other end of the rope, which was still tied to his wrist.

It pulled him right out of his boat and into the water.

"So are you working?"

Hollis blinked and looked in the other direction.

"Not really," he said. "Not right now."

"What *have* you been up to?" said Brian, looking up at him while still hanging on to his ankles. "I never know when I'm going to run into bad old Hollis Kessler anymore. I thought you were at some design company in Back Bay, they did museum displays or something — "

"I was. I quit."

Brian straightened up and patted his stomach.

"I should keep going," he said. "All those Eurobankers think I'm going to be some kind of fat American. You like these sneakers?"

He held one out toward Hollis. It was a complicated patchwork of canvas and rubber and leather.

"They have gel in them."

"Gel, I put on my head," said Hollis, in a fake Yiddish accent. "To put on my feet, who knew?"

Brian looked out across the park at the couple again.

"She sure as fucking hell is cute," he said.

"Oh. I almost forgot — Prasad says hi."

"I know. I saw him too."

"Did he clue you in? Wise you up?" Brian turned and looked at him suddenly. "Set you straight? You know how he's always laying this stuff on people, about what's wrong with them? I bet he had a high old time with you. Not that there's anything wrong with you, cowboy," he added hastily, holding up his hands. "Hey, we *need* you. You're probably the last person I know who isn't — I don't know. Fucking somebody else over for more Experience Points, or something like that. You're not — you know what I mean. Infected."

Formerly a public health inspector, I am now the last human being left alive on earth.

I am Chingachgook. The Last of the Mochicans.

"Prasad. What a penis that guy is. You know what Sree called him? An ABCD: American-Born Confused Deshi. 'Deshi' is supposed to be slang for Indian, or something. You want to jog with me?"

"I can't," said Hollis. "I don't have sneakers."

Brian nodded and looked back over his shoulder at the steep slope that ran down the other side of the hill, down to the road. He pushed his long hair back behind his ears.

"I should go," he said. "Anyway, what are you waiting around here for? Shouldn't you be getting out of here too?"

"Yes," said Hollis. He sighed and looked around for the woman with the ferret, but she was nowhere in sight. "I should try to get back to the building before they do — I can't have him catching me coming in. They'll be a while, though. I think they're having an affair. I should try blackmailing him."

The sun had sunk lower on the horizon, the bottom edge eclipsed by the tops of the trees, and they could look straight at it without squinting. Brian put his hand on Hollis's shoulder for balance and switched to his other leg. Their long shadows ran back into the shadow of the hill and merged with it.

The ball-playing couple had a tiny white subcompact parked on the grass at the other end of the field. They watched the woman as she went through her purse on the hood of the car, looking for her keys.

Pretty. Must destroy.

"So when's your flight?" said Hollis.

"Next Thursday," said Brian. "A week from today. Boston to New York to Stuttgart. On *Lufthansa!*"

He did a Nazi salute, still standing on one leg.

"*Das bestes Airflügt! Ist zo chip!*" He dropped the ankle and stood up straight. "I'll send you a postcard from the Reichstag. Does Steve have your address?"

Hollis nodded. They shook hands.

"Okay, dude."

"Super."

Brian turned away, skipped once or twice as he got going, and jogged off along the crest of the hill. His sneakers pounded softly on the turf. Then he plunged down onto the slope, out of the sunlight, galloping out of control down towards the bottom.

"*Whoa!*"

Hollis watched him run easily through the parking lot and out along the edge of the road, until he disappeared around the bend. He took his hands out of his pockets and blew into them to warm them up.

A car horn blared behind him, a dissonant interval, and there was the sound of skidding tires. He turned around: the white Camry was stopped sideways in the middle of the road, blocking both lanes. An oncoming car had just barely managed to screech to a stop a few feet short of a collision. The driver honked his horn and shook both his hands at Hollis's landlord. Apparently he'd started to pull out without looking, then panicked and changed his mind, and now he was trapped in between.

As Hollis watched, the Camry made a couple of laborious cuts until it could swing back into its lane. His landlord honked his horn back at the other car and accelerated away out of sight.

"God, I have to get out of this city," said Hollis.

The old men in the village sometimes told stories about the Devil-fish, but Tonga had never believed them. Wings thirty feet wide, and horns, and a strange, horrible face on its underside. It only came into the bay at night.

Tonga came up to breathe. The speed with which it was dragging him piled up water against his chest. Already he was even with the sandbar that marked the mouth of the bay.

He was doomed if the Devilfish reached the open sea—it would pull him out into the depths and drown him. There was an old wooden post that stood in the middle of the channel, that had been there for longer than the oldest fisherman in the village could remember, and Tonga felt for it in the darkness.

When he found it he took a deep breath and dove down to the bottom. He made a loop around it with the rope.

His mind was racing. Would the old post hold? Or would he be dragged out to sea, to drown?

By degrees the sunlight became more and more golden and less and less transparent. The wind was turning Hollis's ears pink against his short, razor-cut hair, which was dyed a bright white blond. Afternoon was moving into early evening. He'd locked his bike to a guard barrier made of thick rusty cables, and past the barrier came a thin line of trees, and past them the ground kept sloping away downhill. Far away in the distance he could see the rest of Brookline — bare trees and evergreens and brick buildings all mixed together, still lit up by the sun.

He started jogging down the hill. His shoes slipped on the grass, and he had to catch himself with his hands. When he got to the bottom he was breathing hard, and he had to bend over with his hands on his knees for a few seconds before he could go on.

He was a mysterious figure—arrogant, aristocratic, coldly beautiful, impossible to understand. Even those who tried to draw closer to him, lured by his wealth or the secret of his success, found him enigmatic. Rumors flew around him: bizarre affairs, ruinous addictions, fortunes lost and won, crimes both passionate and dispassionate. His resources of indifference were immense, his capacity for remorse minimal. His contempt for those around him was absolute and matched only by an equal contempt for himself.

Hollis rode back from the park in twilight, pumping hard down the hill, with sunlight flashing behind the trees and casting thick orange bars across the road. There were no sidewalks this far from the center of town, and he rode the very edge of the asphalt, sometimes straying off onto the sandy shoulder. Station wagons stood in the occasional driveways, and every once in a while a powerboat on a trailer under a blue tarp. A film of sweat burned coldly on his forehead.

He stopped at a traffic light, breathing hard, and ran his hands through his hair. The gas station on the corner was lit up with white floodlights, and he could see a clock on the wall through the window: it was almost six. A glowing red-and-black Merit sign towered over him against the blue evening sky. His chest hurt. His breath showed white in the cold fall air.

As he rounded the last corner he passed a few homeless people hanging around in front of the liquor store. The shabby laundromat on the opposite corner was still open. Hollis's apartment building — one of three identical buildings in a row on Commonwealth Avenue in Allston — stood a few hundred yards from a busy intersection. A mile or two outside downtown Boston, Commonwealth was six lanes wide, with train tracks running down the middle. The block of stores across the street had a Parliament billboard mounted on the roof: a scene from the Greek islands, in turquoise blue and alabaster white.

The landlord's car was already there, parked right in front of his building. Hollis spotted it as he coasted up to the steps. There was no point in hurrying anymore. He jumped off his bike, braced himself, and hoisted it up onto his shoulder. A black leather glove lay on the ground by the curb, in an empty parking space, and he glanced down at it as he walked by.

It was lying palm-down, with the thumb folded under it. A tire tread ran across the back. He set the bike down again, bent down, and picked up the glove. Holding it by the fingertips, he slapped it against his thigh a few times to get the sand off and stuffed it in the pocket of his overcoat. It was one of his.

Picking up the bike again, Hollis dug his keys out of his pocket with his free hand and let himself in. The lobby was old and a little run-down: there were scratches on the wallpaper and dents in the walls from years of people moving in and out. He took the stairs, cautiously, lugging his bike with him.

When he got to the fourth floor he peered carefully around the corner out into the hallway.

The landlord stood in front of the door to his apartment. He had to stoop a little as he tried to look in through the peephole the wrong way. Hollis watched as he knocked on it smartly a few times. He called Hollis's name.

Shhhh. I'm hunting wabbits.

Hollis kept climbing, up the stairs two more flights to the top floor, then on up an extra flight of steps, littered with trash and dusted with white plaster powder. The aluminum door at the top was padlocked, but somebody had pried out the nails that held the latch to the doorjamb. With his bike still on his shoulder, Hollis kicked the door open and pushed his way out onto the roof.

From the rooftop the city lights were spread out sparsely across the dark shapes of buildings, like a glittering brush stroke, dominated by pink sodium streetlights. The roof wasn't built to be walked on: it was made out of nothing more than overlapping scraps of tar paper laid out over something that gave a little when Hollis put his weight on it. Here and there an assortment of vents and ducts and boxy air conditioners poked up at random. There was no railing around the edge, just a low brick wall at about knee height.

A wrought-iron ladder led down to the fire escape. Hollis walked over to it, unshouldered his bike, and locked it to the top rung with a heavy steel chain. Taking a deep breath, he grabbed the top rung with both hands and swung himself out over the edge.

Danger, Will Robinson! Danger!

The concrete courtyard wheeled around under him, six stories below. He'd never been down there. An old stone birdbath lay propped up in a corner, half filled with brown rainwater. It didn't even occur to Hollis until he was already outside his own window that it might be locked, but when he tried the sash it opened.

He bent down to look in. His bedroom looked weirdly unfamiliar from this angle. Warm air blew out into his face, and past him out into the chilly late afternoon.

Hollis took off his combat boots, set them carefully beside him on the cold wrought-iron grille, and crawled in onto the desktop in his socks. He brushed against a stack of paperbacks with his hip; it slumped gracefully over onto the floor. He lived in a studio apartment: one big room, a bathroom, and a kitchen annex, with white plaster walls and a high ceiling. Books, clothes, cards, floppy disks, CDs, tapes, comic books, and bottles of pills littered the floor. Hollis went into the bathroom and turned on the hot-water faucet in the bath. He came back out into the bedroom and sat down on the edge of the bed.

The light on his answering machine was blinking. He pressed the play button.

"Hollis, it's Peters."

A car honked in the background — he was calling from a pay phone, or a cell phone. Somebody else said something Hollis couldn't understand.

"Listen," he said, "Blake and I have a car. We're coming over to your place, and then we're going to drink your booze and make fun of the Establishment. It's like the Merry Pranksters all over again. We're — "

The message cut off with a *beep*. By now, huge white billows of steam were swirling out through the open bathroom door and dissolving into the cooler air in the bedroom. Hollis was still wearing his overcoat. He shrugged out of it and let it fall on the floor.

The rope vibrated with the strain, surging with the beats of the manta's wings. Tonga's lungs ached for air. His eyes were shut tight against the stinging salt pressure.

Then, all at once, the rope went slack.

Slowly, Tonga unwound it from around the post and kicked his way back up to the surface, through the warm blackness of the water. His legs felt weak. He took a deep breath, holding on to the old, worm-eaten wood. His palms stung where the rope had cut them.

Across the water the friendly lights of the village still glowed along the shore. Tonga turned the other way and looked out to sea. It was dark, and he couldn't see the horizon. He started swimming back towards his tiny skiff, which was still drifting by itself in the calm bay.

Tonga had learned his lesson: he would never go fishing alone at night again.

The last of the weak sunlight slanted in through the lowered blinds. The machine beeped again.

"Hollis," said a woman's voice. "Look, Hollis, is this still you? It's Eileen Cavanaugh."

A heavy click on the line interrupted her — her call waiting. When her voice came back she was talking in double-time so as not to miss the other call.

"Look, if this *is* your answering machine — and why you can't have a normal outgoing message like a normal person is beyond me" — the call waiting clicked again — "I know you — "

Hollis reached over and turned the volume all the way down.

Suddenly it was very quiet in the apartment. He went over and retrieved his boots from the fire escape. Before he closed the window, he dug the lost glove out of the pocket of his overcoat and laid it out on the windowsill to dry.

"I never saw that glove before in my life," she said irritably.

She stood there looking down at it, twisting it nervously between her fingers.

I went to join her at the window, and together we stared down at the green park of my sumptuous estate. Somehow the view was oppressive to me, and I rang for the curtains to be closed.

I waited for the servants to go before I spoke.

"I met him today, you know," I said. "On the moor."

"Oh?" she replied coldly. "Riding to hounds, were you?"

With the light from the candles behind it, her lustrous blond hair looked dark.

"Everything's out in the open now," I said. "I know all about it."

"I know." A flush rose to her high cheekbones. "I saw him, too."

Her mouth had a distinctive shape which I had always particularly relished, an unusually full lower lip deriving from her Hapsburg ancestry. I went to the table and poured myself some wine, but my hands were unsteady and a few drops splashed onto the white linen of the tablecloth.

"He'll be leaving soon," I said. "He told me all about it: an official appointment in the capital. King and country, that sort of thing. I expect he'll be by for you in the night, or some such heroics."

Before she spoke, she rang for someone to come and open the curtains again.

"Don't be ridiculous," she said.

I had this dream where we were all on the Enterprise, *from* Star Trek.

Something happens to the Earth, and it blows up, and all these different cities fly off into space. Each one lands on a different planet. We decide we're going to go find out what happened to Boston, so we fly to the planet where Boston ended up after the explosion, and it turns out to be an ice planet. Everything's covered over with these deep, powdery snowdrifts. We drive around for a while looking for people we know, and finally we find some people who were friends with Counselor Troi. She gets out and decides to stay there with them.

Then we're driving back out of the city, back to the Enterprise, *and* we're going around a corner, and our *truck skids off the road into a snowdrift. Somehow the door comes open, and I get thrown out into the snow. Captain Picard falls out on top of me. He gets up right away, but for some reason I can't get up after him. I'm lying there in the snowdrift, and he gets back into the truck and closes the door. The truck starts up again, and they all drive away without me.*

After a while I get up again. I start walking back the other way, back towards Boston, to see if I can find Counselor Troi. I walk for hours and hours, and the road curves through a forest, then out across a wide, empty plain.

It's getting on towards dusk when I finally see the ruined skyline of Boston in the distance, through a scrim of falling snow, with a few lights still on among the crumbled-looking skyscrapers. There's somebody coming up the road towards me from out of the city, and when she gets closer I recognize her. It's Counselor Troi.

She comes up to me without saying anything, and we look into each other's eyes. Powdery snow swirls across the white crust and settles into her wavy dark hair, where it melts. I press my communicator badge.

"Away Team to Enterprise. *Come in,* Enterprise.*"*

We listen, but nobody answers. I press it again.

It's busy.

The door buzzer went off. Hollis opened his eyes.

He was curled up under the comforter in the middle of his bed. The lights had been off when he fell asleep, and now the apartment was dark. The radiator hissed. Condensed moisture beaded on the insides of the windows, behind the venetian blinds. Books and clothes lay all over everything. He could see the white shape of the Sunday Help Wanted section of the *Globe* spread out on the floor.

Hollis sighed and stretched under the blanket. There was a poster of Brenghel's *Icarus* on the opposite wall, but it was too dark to see the figures on it. The air was warm and humid. Whoever it was buzzed again, and he sat up, and his eyes filled with blobs of color. The clock on his desk said 7:50 P.M. In the pinkish light coming in through the windows from a streetlight he found an embroidered bathrobe on the floor and put it on. He went over to the wall panel and held down the DOOR button.

When he was done, Hollis flopped back down on the bed and pulled the blanket up over his legs. Clasping his hands behind his head, he looked up at the ceiling and took a deep breath. Through his window he could see into the hallway of the building next door, which was a modern high-rise condo. Fluorescent lights flickered on and off along the ceiling. A woman passed by, holding both her hands at the back of her head, adjusting her French braid as she walked.

After a minute there were footsteps outside in the hall, and Hollis heard people talking.

"Why does he even live here?"

"It looks like one of those existential heavy metal videos. With some old guy in a cell."

Hollis got up and opened the door without waiting for them to knock.

"Hello, Hollis," said Peters crisply.

"Hey guys."

Peters was tall, with broad shoulders and shoulder-length wavy brown hair, and he wore tiny round glasses with metal rims. He had on a gray overcoat, a green flannel shirt, and jeans with a blue ink stain on the pocket. Blake was shorter, and he was dressed immaculately: an expensive suit jacket and pants with a white T-shirt. He had a neat blond goatee.

Peters took a step inside and looked around.

"Christ, it's dark in here," he said. Hollis closed the door. "Don't you have any more lights?"

"Nope."

Peters walked over to the desk, picking his way through the stuff on the floor.

"Pip pip," he said. "Don't just stand there moping, Hollis. Cheerio. Jesus, look at this place, it looks like a squirrel's nest."

Hollis followed him, rubbing the sleep out of his eyes.

"Quit with the snappy patter, will you?"

Peters swiveled the desk lamp up so it faced the ceiling, then snatched his hand away and shook it.

"Fucking Christ!" he said.

"I knew somebody named Christ once," said Blake, leaning against the doorframe. "He said it 'Krist,' like you say 'whist.'"

"Blake, you don't have the conversation God gave a goat," said Peters. "Listen, I had this dream last night—I forgot to tell you this, Blake."

He spun the desk chair around and sat down on it backwards, facing them.

"It was about me and Axl Rose," he said. "We were in this cross-country motorcycle chase. The government was seeking us in connection with some unspecified but probably heinous crime. Which we probably actually did commit, but for some good reason that we just couldn't explain in terms that would make it legally acceptable. Anyway, it was just us and these guys in suits, all just blasting down the highway after each other on motorcycles. Blue sky, blazing sun, waving wheat. Finally they catch up with us in this huge swamp, where we're sort of cornered. There's hordes of police cars blocking off the road—it's just like the end of *Thelma and Louise*. Lots of flashing lights. Police sharpshooters lying on the ground and stuff. You can see these swamp plants waving in the wind, all around us.

"Everybody's really quiet. Axl slowly takes out his shotgun and fires two shots, straight down into the swamp. He pulls the trigger a couple of extra times, just to make sure everybody sees that the gun's empty. Click click. Everybody relaxes. Then, in slow motion, he takes out his lighter, and he lights it. It turns out there's all this flammable swamp gas in the swamp, and he's deliberately releasing it by making these holes in, like, the upper layer of the mud, with his gun. So then he throws his lighter down into the swamp, and all the swamp gas explodes. He and I get away in the confusion."

There were a few seconds of silence.

"Is that it?" said Hollis.

"At least there's a happy ending," said Blake.

"I just keep wondering if that would really work."

"What are you guys doing all the way out here, anyway?" said Hollis. He went over to the bed and started straightening out the comforter. "I was just going to try calling you."

"Blake has a car," Peters said. "I had to take back some jeans that were too small, but the place was closed. You weren't asleep, were you?"

"No, I got up early and went over to that park in Brookline. Where'd you get a car?"

"It's mine," said Blake.

"What kind?"

"Lexus."

"Jeezus."

"You should be careful, Hollis," said Peters, swiveling himself around in circles on the desk chair. "One day you're going to go to bed and not wake up for like, twenty years."

"I hope I do."

"Why don't you just kill yourself?"

Hollis started folding up the futon into a couch, holding his robe closed with one hand.

"I cannot self-terminate," he said, in a Schwarzenegger accent.

Blake went over to the other side of the futon to help him. When they'd wrestled it into its upright position, he sat down and clasped his hands behind his head.

"Let's put on some music."

"My stereo's broken. There's something wrong with the power in this building — the wiring's old."

"Hmmm," said Peters, looking around the room with a bored expression on his face. "Quite a three-pipe problem, Watson."

Hollis's short hair was still standing on end. The desk lamp cast a glowing lozenge on the ceiling, leaving the corners of the room dark. The only other light came from the window, except for a line of light under the door from the hall.

It was a brisk evening in early September, and my celebrated colleague and I were passing a quiet evening in his room when the landlady announced a young woman waiting to speak to us on the landing.

Peters got up and walked over to a bookcase standing against the wall.

"I was over at Alison's the other day," he said. "She has two copies of *The Gulag Archipelago*. Can you imagine that? What would you do with two copies of *The Gulag Archipelago*? Can you even imagine anybody actually reading that book?"

He took one down at random and started looking through it.

"Got anything to drink?" he said.

"No," said Hollis.

"What about food?"

"Just some Corn Pops."

"Hell."

"They're fat-free."

Peters looked up and snapped the book shut.

"Okay, check this out. You fall out of an airplane — it's some kind of skyjacking gone awry. The bomb goes off, there's a hole in the wall, and you get sucked out by the difference in air pressure. You're unhurt, but you're falling through the air at like, terminal velocity."

"Right."

"It's like one of those Ripley's things. I was thinking about this last night. Somebody falls out of a plane and lands on something soft, like a haystack or something — it happens all the time. Or a bog. Or they just fall into the sea or something and they survive."

"I hear the wind tears off all your clothes while you're in the air," said Blake. "If you aren't wearing special skydiving clothes."

He thoughtfully nudged a copy of *Wired* along the floor with the toe of his boot.

"At plane-crash sites you have all these naked bodies lying around."

"Peters, you're standing on my overcoat," said Hollis. "My shades are in there."

Peters took a step backwards and picked up the overcoat. He held it up by the collar and slapped it a few times, then dropped it in the corner.

"That coat is getting really horrible, Hollis," he said. "By the way, I have plans for you this weekend. Don't let me forget. Did you follow up on that tip David gave you — the Houghton Mifflin thing? He asked me about it."

"Tomorrow."

"I would, if I were you. Just go by their office. It wouldn't be a real job, you know. And so what if it was, anyway? They're going to throw you out of here pretty soon, if you don't pay some rent. It's not like you'd be breaking a moral principle or anything, is it? Christ, do you *ever* open these windows?"

He walked over to the futon and cleared off the windowsill behind it, which was covered with an assortment of bits and pieces — coins, glasses, empty tape cases, a screwdriver, a wine bottle with a candle stuck in it.

"It's like a fucking hyperbaric chamber in here."

"What the hell *is* a hyperbaric chamber?" said Blake.

When Peters got the window open, it turned out there was an old storm window in place behind it. He got up on his knees on the futon, fumbled around for the latches, and heaved up on it. Nothing happened. He braced himself and tried again, this time putting his considerable weight behind it. There was an intense, crunching noise, and instead of sliding up the window jumped out of its frame and flew straight out into the air. Peters grabbed at it once and missed.

It shattered faintly on the concrete of the courtyard. A gust of cold air blew in through the empty frame.

Blake started laughing helplessly. Peters looked around quickly, then ducked his head back into the room.

He mimed dusting off his hands.

"Sorry about that," he said.

"You should have seen your face," said Blake, dabbing at his eyes.

"Don't worry about it," said Hollis languidly. "I don't pay for heat."

Peters looked a little shaken. He took a thin black wallet out of his back pocket.

"I guess I should give you some money or something. I'm really sorry about that. Jesus, why don't they make those things out of plastic?"

"Uh-oh," said Blake. "Maybe it was an antique."

Hollis waved him away, but Peters took out a ten-dollar bill and put it on his desk, saying:

"Buy yourself something nice."

"Have you guys ever heard of hand models?" said Hollis. He

held up his hands with the backs outward, like a surgeon waiting to be gowned. "One of those people who model watches and pens and stuff? I don't know what else. Rings. It's cool—they wear gloves when they eat. They get their hands insured for millions of dollars. And how would you even know if you were one? Statistically speaking, you'd think everybody would have *some* part of their body that was worth modeling with. It's really just a question of figuring out which one it is."

"Don't quit your day job," said Blake.

"Look at his hands—like a child's hands!"

Wonderingly, the peasants took the stranger's hands in their own thick, callused fingers, eyeing him with a newfound respect.

"Never meant for toil, that's sure!"

The man who seemed to be their leader stepped forward.

"Stranger," he said, "I wote well ye're of an higher blood than we wend ye were."

"So what about this weekend?" said Peters. "Are you doing anything?"

"Nothing so far. The jury's still out."

"Does anybody have a cigarette?"

Hollis shook his head. There was a broken piece of mirror leaned against the wall, and he looked down at his reflection, surreptitiously.

"Why?" he said. "Are you going to New York?"

"Some friends of the family are going away. They have a house in Dover. I thought maybe we could go hang out there for a few days."

"What's in Dover?"

"Not much. It's like a gated community—everything's privately owned. All the roads are private and stuff."

"It's the second-richest town in Massachusetts," said Blake. "Fun fact."

"Out in the sticks?" said Hollis. "I don't know. What's the first-richest?"

Peters shrugged.

"I guess it's pretty rural. About forty minutes out of Boston. You should see the house, though, it's very cool: hot tub, weight room, everything. Cable. Nintendo. A laser-disc player. We can put in some serious screen time. There's like a million fucking rooms in it, too."

Hollis got up off the futon and went out into the anteroom by the door, which had a tiny closet. Out of sight of the others he picked out a pair of clean boxers and stepped into them, pulling them up underneath the robe.

"That's all I was thinking," Peters called from the other room, raising his voice. "We can't really have people over there. They'll be gone till next Friday."

"Are you house-sitting for them?" Hollis called back.

"Not exactly."

"Oh." He paused. "What *are* you doing, exactly?"

"Just using their stuff, I guess."

"Are they going to know?"

"Not really."

"Why not?"

"Well, I don't think they'd like it."

Hollis came out and stood in the doorframe, in his socks and boxers. They were green, with little white whales on them.

"So we're supposed to break into their house?"

"Relax. I have a key. If we're careful they'll never find out—they're overseas." He yawned. "Well, they're in the Caribbean."

Hollis watched him, feeling with one foot for the opening of a pair of jeans. Peters stood up and went back over to the book-case. He took out a book and looked at it in the half-darkness.

"Did you know that J. D. Salinger has two whole novels, brand-new, locked up in a bank vault somewhere in Vermont? He won't publish them."

"Why not?" said Blake, from the couch.

"I don't know. Some hippy-dippy Zen-type reason."

"What's their name?" said Hollis. "The family friends, I mean."

"Donnelly."

Hollis thought for a second.

"Didn't we use their Cape house once? Why don't we go there?"

"No," said Peters. He made a face. "I'd never go there now. There's something about beaches in the fall—I can't stand it. Dead horseshoe crabs. Old people with metal detectors. Heaps of fucking . . . I don't know. Whatever it is. Kelp. Makes you want to kill yourself."

He looked up. His glasses flashed in the light from the desk lamp. He put his hands in his pockets and took out a pack of Marlboros and a book of matches. With a tricky little sleight-of-hand gesture, he opened the matchbook and lit a match with one hand.

"Besides, I hate that stupid prefabricated cottage. It looks like a displaced motel room. You start feeling like fucking Alfred J. Prufrock out there. Life's passing you by, I'm so insignificant, etc., etc. There was a movie I saw once, about these guys who were desperately trying to kill this alien who was morphing weirdly all over the place in this research station somewhere up above the Arctic Circle. Some really revolting special effects. It was a trip. Anyway, at the way end there's just these two guys sitting in the middle of nowhere, in this Arctic wasteland, with their whole camp destroyed, and you basically know they're going to die, even though they've just saved the world from this alien. It's Kurt Russell, actually. Kind of like a metaphor for his whole career, in a way."

"Not since *Stargate*," said Blake. "Now he's B-list again."

"You don't mind if I smoke, do you?"

"No," said Hollis.

"Knock yourself out," said Blake.

Peters watched the match flame meditatively, as it dwindled down to a little blue pearl and finally vanished in a puff of smoke.

"I need something to ash in," he said.

"There's a can next to your foot."

"Anyway, it's probably all closed up," he went on. "The cottage. Besides, I doubt if I could get the key, except if it's in the Dover house."

"I don't know," said Hollis. "The whole thing sounds a little weird."

"Well, look, go or don't go, I don't care. Don't spoil it for me with your, like, moral qualms." He rolled his eyes. "What else do you have to do? Anyway, think what Mr. Donnelly made last year — probably about five hundred thousand? You probably live on about *ten* thousand a year, at this point. Is that social justice? These are troubled times, Hollis: we have to look at the underlying causes. Is it for us to settle questions of right and wrong? Kill 'em all and let God sort 'em out."

He dragged on his cigarette.

"Besides," he said, exhaling, "it's not like they'll press charges or anything if they catch us. They know me."

"Close that window, would you, Blake?" said Hollis. "It's fucking freezing in here."

A muscle in his chest started to twitch involuntarily, under the bathrobe, and he pulled the lapels around him more tightly.

He looked up at the white Arctic sky.
"That's what we get for trying to save the world," he said wryly.
Powdery snow swirled across the white crust.

"How're you going to get a key?" said Hollis.

"We have to sneak in and get it. There's one door in the back that they always leave unlocked. It's their Achilles' heel. Their tragic flaw. We'll have to get kind of pumped up for this, Hollis, it's a punk thing. Sid Vicious, man. *Épatez les bourgeois. Ne travaillez jamais.* Anyway, aren't you sick of hanging around this fucking slum? I sure as hell am."

Peters turned around and faced the other window, with his hands clasped behind his back. He was broad enough that his shoulders filled the frame, obscuring Hollis's view. His hair made a wavy silhouette against the light outside.

"What do you pay on this place, anyway?" he said, after a while.

"Four twenty-five."

"That's not bad," said Blake.

"Anyway, what else do you have to do?" Peters turned back around to face them. "You need something to tell your grandkids about, when you're old and horrible and drooling and nobody loves you anymore. They'll have a spare set of house keys somewhere — we'll just take those and go back tomorrow night when they're gone. They'll never catch us. 'All that which is necessary for life is the rightful property of the people.' *Comme a dit* Robespierre."

"Oh, *très bon*," said Blake. "Did you just make that up?"

"You know, Vanessa Redgrave used to leave the door of her house unlocked when she went out. She said all her stuff was supposed to belong to the people."

"Why don't you just go over to her place?" said Blake, stroking his goatee.

"Who's Vanessa Redgrave?" said Hollis.

"Their son is doing some kind of internship or something at Hallmark, too," Peters went on. "As in Hallmark cards. I hear he's going out with the heiress to the Honeywell fortune, or whatever's left of it. A real fucking comer, anyway. He and I were playfellows, in our youth."

He looked up.

"Anyway, if we're going it has to be tonight. Don't you want to get out of your bubble for a change?"

"We fear change."

"What ever happened to boys in bubbles?" said Hollis. "Aren't they news anymore? Are you going, Blake?"

He shook his head.

"I shouldn't even hang around with you guys. This is the kind of stuff that comes up at confirmation hearings."

Hollis went back into the anteroom to finish dressing. He let the robe slip off his shoulders. Looking through a heap of clean clothes on the floor of the closet, he found a white tuxedo shirt with the collar ripped off and a dark red suit jacket. As he put on the jacket, he felt something in the inside pocket and took it out: a piece of onionskin typing paper folded in thirds. There was a block of text on it, typed with a manual typewriter — the whole rectangle of words was palpably impressed into the paper.

"She's still writing you poems?" said Eileen. She looked over at him, then reached out and took the piece of paper.

"It's not to me just because she gave it to me."

"Don't you think it's time you and she had a frank conversation, Hollis? I'm trying to make an honest man of you here."

She walked over to the couch, sat down on the arm, and flopped backwards onto the old vinyl seat cushions. Air whooshed out of them, a little maelstrom of dust in the sunlight from the window. Her dress slid part of the way up her pale thighs. The folded piece of paper rested on her stomach.

She stared up at the ceiling, blankly.

"I can't read it," she said.

"Is there anything to drink?" said Peters. He stepped out of the bedroom into the kitchen alcove. Blake was looking through the stacks of tapes on the floor.

"You just asked me that," said Hollis. "There's water."

He heard the sound of water running and Peters shifting dishes in the sink. Then it stopped. Peters opened the freezer.

"Jesus," he said. "You're holding out on me, Hollis — there's gin back here."

"Oh. Sorry, I forgot it was there."

"Look at this stuff: Crystal Palace. You want some?"

"Maybe a shot. With some water."

"The police are so weird," Peters said, over the sound of his mixing drinks. "I was watching some of those transit police guys the other day. Just hanging around. Pounding the beat. I have this theory that about a hundred years from now it's just going to be different kinds of police, fighting it out in the nuclear rubble — nomadic tribes of highway patrolmen and state troopers, roaming around in the ruins of our nation's shattered infrastructure. Troglodyte subway police who surface at night to steal our children and raise them as their own."

There was a long moment of silence.

"Or not," said Blake, from the bedroom.

"Police are on the way out," said Hollis. "I read it on Usenet. In the future it's supposed to be all multinational corporations. *Zaibatsus*. Then they'll all have their own private paramilitary forces."

"Yeah. True." Peters stirred. "I guess that nuclear holocaust stuff is pretty *passé* anyway."

He did a fake computer-voice: "*Let's play* . . . *Global Thermonuclear War.*"

When he came back into the room he brought the drinks with him, a gin and water for himself and a shot and a glass of water for Hollis. He sat down heavily on the futon next to Blake, and Hollis came in from the anteroom and sat at the desk. From outside in the street the sound of the trolley drifted in, rumbling past with its bell ringing.

"What are you thinking about, Hollis?" said Eileen.

He looked up at the ceiling without answering.

"You know," he said, after a few seconds, "whenever you say something incredibly cliché like that, I can't help thinking about all the other people you've probably said it to after you had sex with them."

"Well, I never think about them."

"I think my favorite's that one you met on the subway."

"Christ, Hollis, must you be so psychotically fucking jealous all the fucking time?" she said, sitting up, the sheet slipping down off her bare breasts. "God knows you've slept with some lovely individuals in your own time, and you don't hear me whining about it!"

She flopped back down again, and the bed creaked.

"Besides, I haven't seen him in years."

"You're right you haven't seen him," said Hollis. "He's dead. I killed him."

Blake yawned.

"Damn," he said, rubbing his eyes. "I didn't go to bed till around five this morning. I saw a roach in my room and I couldn't go to sleep. The sun's rising, and I'm completely naked, on my hands and knees under the kitchen table, with a rolled-up newspaper."

"That's a pretty picture," said Peters. He sipped his drink. "Look, are you coming tomorrow?"

"Why don't we ask some girls?" said Hollis.

"Girls ruin everything."

"There's no point without any girls." Hollis was buttoning his shirt slowly, with one hand, staring off into space.

"Let's ask Sarah and Ashley and them," he said.

"We'll talk about it later. Come on, we're going to catch *Metropolis* at nine. You want to come?"

"Seen it. Look, we're going to have to call them tonight if we want them to come."

"They won't come anyway, Hollis. Forget it. Think about something else. Take your mind off it. Look, why don't you meet us after the movie? We're all going to the GT."

"What about Emily?"

"Emily? That girl." Peters snorted. "She's too cheap to meter."

As they walked over to the door, something heavy hit the floor upstairs with a *bang*, and the light fixture rattled.

"Jesus!" Peters said, looking up. "Look, why don't you call her yourself? You're coming, though, tonight? To Dover?"

"Tonight?" Hollis frowned. "Why?"

"Why? How soon they forget. To get the key, that's why."

"I guess so."

He snapped open the locks.

"Don't fall asleep," said Peters, stepping out into the hall.

In the darkness of the garden I could dimly make out rows of giant pods, each one visibly beginning to take on human form.

"Don't fall asleep!" he shouted. "That's when they get you!"

"Why don't you call Alison?" said Blake.

"Oh, that was a droll little affair," said Peters. "Forget about it. You know what women are like? They're like those long, skinny blocks you get in Tetris, the ones made out of four blocks straight in a row. First when you need them you can't get any, then when you don't need them anymore they're fucking everywhere and you don't know what to do with them.

"Every once in a while I ask myself if Alison and I are ever actually going to get together, and of course the answer is no, and it's upsetting, so I quit thinking about it, and soon I get back some of my self-esteem, and then I squander it all again running around after her. It's kind of a cycle. Good thing I'm getting wasted tonight or this might actually start to bother me. Midnight, right? The movie's at the other theater, down on JFK Boulevard. Not the main one."

"She ain't worth the salt in yer tears," said Blake.

"Courage," I said. The young adjutant came up with his horse.

He glanced back at me piercingly—his vision was unusually acute—and a little sadly.

"As for that, mon vieux," he said, "je n'en ai rien."

He swung up into the saddle. It was the last time I was to see him alive.

Hollis waited at the door while Peters and Blake walked away down the hall, backwards, facing back towards him, their shoes echoing loudly on the tiled floor.

"See you there," he said.

CHAPTER 3

Hollis stepped down from the rear doors of the bus. The doors folded closed behind him, and the bus roared and pulled away. He smelled the warm, invisible exhaust roiling around him in the darkness. The street was almost deserted, and bits of crumpled trash rustled along the pavement in the wind. The galleries of shops and cafés were mostly closed. Ahead of him, five or six blocks up the street, shone the lights of Harvard Square.

The temperature had dropped, and he pulled his coat around him more tightly. He could make out the white light of the tiny marquee where he was supposed to meet Peters and Blake, and he walked towards it. The sidewalk was pieced together unevenly, its old bricks slowly subsiding into the mud. Passing a café with a sunken patio, he looked down at the stacks of white wire furniture. A single long chain ran through the chairs and tables, one by one, forming a big loop that was closed with a big steel padlock.

The glass doors of the cinema were locked from the inside. A red velvet rope had been slung across all but one of them, and a woman in a white blouse and a red bow tie was wiping down the candy counter with a damp sponge. Hollis stood outside and looked at the *Metropolis* poster, which was on display in a lighted box. A handsome hero and his winsome lover, who seemed to be made out of some kind of metal, embraced in the shadow of a futuristic city that loomed up over them in the background.

"Hollis. Hollister!" Peters was standing behind him. "I've been calling your name for like half an hour."

"Sorry, dude," said Hollis. "Like, I was spaced."

They joined the crowd of people leaving the cinema in twos and threes. Peters walked quickly, hands in the pockets of his jeans, while Hollis tagged along after him.

"I have to start getting more sleep," he said.

"If you get any more sleep we're going to have to put you on an IV."

They separated to walk around a strolling couple. A green-and-white ambulance stood idling at the curb, and Hollis peeked in one of the small rear windows as they passed. The driver sat in the front seat, studying a clipboard by the light of the dome light.

"I always try to see what's going on inside," said Hollis. "I don't know why. I'd probably be appalled if I ever did."

"Probably somebody got overexcited at Spoken Word Night at the Fern Bar."

"What happened to Blake? I thought he was with you."

"He took off before the end. Had to do something."

"He left before it was over?" Hollis wrinkled his nose. "How can he do that?"

Peters shrugged. "Nerves of steel, I guess," he said. "You ever been there?" He pointed out a basement Thai restaurant. "The waiter tried to pick up my date. I think he thought I was gay. Oh, look, can you cover me tonight? All I have is ten dollars."

Hollis thought for a second.

"I guess so."

"*Domo arigato*, Mr. Roboto."

To be precise, Doctor, I am not a robot, I am an android—a sophisticated computer endowed with the form of a human simulacrum, and capable of many human functions.

Hollis blew into his hands.

"Who's going to be there tonight, anyway?" he said.

"I'm not sure. Basil, probably."

"God. I hate that guy."

The wind came up from behind them, from the direction of the river, stirring the dead leaves in the street. Bars were closing. People were making their way home. Hollis watched a cleaning woman moving around in the office windows above a row of stores.

An orange sawhorse was set up in the middle of the sidewalk, where some bricks were missing.

"In the student revolt in Paris they ripped up the cobblestones out of the streets," said Peters as he walked around it. "I guess they threw them at people or something. Maybe they were for the barricades. Anyway, there was all this nice yellow beach sand under them, so people started saying 'Under the Pavement, the Beach.' It turned into a big slogan in the sixties."

"Them crazy French."

Peters looked through his jacket pockets for a cigarette, then reached over and put his hand in Hollis's pocket. He pulled out the lining, along with a clump of lint. It was empty.

"Don't you smoke anymore?"

"I never smoked," said Hollis, stuffing the lining back in.

"You smoke pot."

"Pot is easier. Anyway, I don't anymore — I keep getting the paranoid trip."

Peters snorted. "Maybe you can be a lung model."

Two young women turned the corner out of a side street and walked ahead of them, in the same direction. Both were slender and stylishly dressed, and Peters put his hand on Hollis's arm. He pointed and made a gurgling noise in his throat. They passed a little green public park, a rectangular swath of grass with a few trees and a memorial statue. The grass showed some bare patches. A few couples still sat there in the dark, huddled together on benches.

"I think I know one of them," said Peters, jerking his head at the two women. "Oh, guess who called me yesterday — Evan Goldsmith. I was just going out last night, and he calls me up out of the blue and asks me if I get Channel 5. So I say, sure. So he says, well, I can't get it, so could you turn on your TV for a while — the Tony awards were on or something — so he can listen to it *over the phone.*"

He laughed.

"He was still on when I got home."

"He's insane," said Hollis. "There's something wrong with him. He once watched *Predator* all the way through on cable, scrambled."

This close to Harvard Square the street was still full of traffic, even though it was after midnight. Peters and Hollis had to wait to cross the street. The two women were waiting too.

"Eleanor," said Peters, after a second, and one of the women started. She turned around. She was tall, at least as tall as Hollis, and she had a scarf wrapped around her head that made her short brown hair stand straight up.

"Oh, hi, Peters," she said, putting her hand on her chest. "You scared me. How are you? I thought you graduated."

She smiled sweetly, showing her teeth, which stuck out slightly. She wore a dark blue overcoat with a man's suit jacket underneath. She'd tucked a scarf into her collar.

"I did," said Peters. "I'm teaching for Professor Delahay now."

"I thought Delahay went to Rutgers."

"Not till the spring. It's a dual appointment."

Peters put his hand behind Hollis's shoulders.

"This is my bosom friend Hollis."

They shook hands.

"Eleanor Garr."

Peters turned to the other woman, who introduced herself as Kirsten. She was short, and plain, with straight blond hair cut in a China Chop. The light changed, and traffic started going the other way, but they didn't cross.

"So how's Jason?" said Peters. "Is he still working for Giuliani?"

Eleanor nodded. "He hates it." She wrinkled up her nose. "He was up this weekend. They're sending him to the Carolinas."

"What are you guys doing right now?"

"Oh, God knows. Probably going home."

"I have midterms all this week," said Kirsten. She turned her head to one side, slightly languorously, and looked over at Eleanor. "We were just at the Casablanca. I think Ron Howard was there — I think I recognized him."

A lock of Eleanor's bangs had escaped the scarf and was falling down over her high forehead.

"You're not related to Teri Garr, are you?" Hollis said, looking at her. "You look a little like her."

"Do I?" She flashed him a smile and raised a hand to her cheek experimentally. "God, I hope not."

"That's a morbid idea, Hollis," said Peters. "Listen, we're going to be at the GT for a while — you guys should drop by."

The WALK signal was gone again, but the street was empty, and Eleanor stepped off the curb.

"Maybe we will," she said. She smiled again. "See you later."

"See you," said Peters.

"Nice to meet you, Hollis."

Hollis and Peters stayed behind on the curb watching them go, then Peters steered them down the side street, away from the Square, to where the streets got narrower and darker.

"Why did you have to say that thing about Teri Garr?" said Peters. "Here I am introducing you to a beautiful woman — "

"Oh, for God's sake," said Hollis. "She's an undergraduate — she must be eighteen years old."

"So? You're only twenty-three," said Peters. "Love is ageless. Besides, you're probably the most undergraduate person I know. And I know a lot of undergraduates."

In the row of darkened storefronts there was one lighted window, a café where people were loading up on coffee and pastries after a night of drinking.

"How would you feel if somebody said you looked like Scott Bakula, or something? Or Bronson Pinchot? God, no wonder Eileen dumped you."

"Teri Garr's pretty well-preserved," said Hollis calmly. "Anyway, I broke up with Eileen, not the other way around, if you want to know the truth."

"That's what they all say," said Peters.

The side street led them to a wide plaza set with curvy, impressionistic stone benches. A few skinny saplings had been planted there, in square plots. A couple of buskers were still playing — two tough-looking women sitting facing each other on stools, an acoustic guitarist and a drummer. The music was very soft, almost inaudible, and the drummer bent her head down to listen more intently to the guitar. Hollis hugged his overcoat tight around him. He stopped and picked up a schedule out of a plastic milk crate sitting in front of a movie theater.

"She has a boyfriend, anyway," Peters said, after a while. "Eleanor does. He's a real nebbish. Which reminds me — did you hear about Peter Bracey?"

They stopped to wait at another crossing.

"He got a job writing for Letterman. One day he's sitting around in his apartment, making jokes about snot. No job, no furniture, no money, no nothing. Now he's making a hundred thousand a year."

"Jesus Christ," said Hollis.

"He was on the *Lampoon. Full* of fucking connections."

The Ghost Town Café was on the corner of a dark alley that was closed off to cars by two metal posts set in the pavement. Hollis and Peters walked down it in step, silently, with their hands in their pockets. The alley was in the process of being metamorphosed into a pedestrian shopping zone: they'd replaced the asphalt with cobblestones, and a nearby department store had set up a row of display windows. A tangle of wrought-iron fire escapes still hung ominously overhead, and farther along a big blue Dumpster was overflowing in an alcove. The cobblestones were wet, and they gleamed in the light from a single streetlight.

A group of three was already waiting for them outside the GT. Peters waved as they came up, and Blake gave a cursory wave back.

"Hey hey, it's the *Manqués*," said Basil, who was tall and thin, with high cheekbones. His short dark hair was cut in a Spartacus cut.

"It's fucking freezing out here," said Rob, a redheaded undergraduate with a long Roman nose. His ears were almost perfectly perpendicular to his head. "I'm going in."

Blake had already pushed through the door. The interior of the GT was supposed to look like a Mexican cantina: everything was made of rough unfinished wood, and there were paintings of cactuses on the walls and neon Corona and Dos Equis signs hanging in the windows. About half the tables were full, and there was a noisy crowd around the bar. They sat down in a booth. Peters collected everybody's coats and piled them up in an empty seat.

"Your coat, sir?" he said, turning to Hollis.

"Be careful. There's a check in the inside pocket."

"Is there?" said Peters. "Let me guess — Mom's life insurance paid off."

"I liquidated my last stocks today," said Hollis. "My grandmother gave them to me when I was born. It was kind of depressing, actually — kind of like that scene in *Risky Business*, when Tom Cruise cashes all those bonds to pay for a call girl."

"You slept with a call girl?" said Rob.

"What'd you make?" said Blake.

"Not very much. Six or seven hundred. I only had a few shares left."

A tired-looking waiter came up to the table, and they ordered a round of drinks.

"Wait," said Peters, when the waiter was gone. "Wait. That can't possibly be true. You hardly even got up today."

"So? Okay, I went yesterday."

"So why didn't you just say you went yesterday?"

"I don't know," said Hollis. "It just seemed simpler."

"Has it ever occurred to you that you're a compulsive liar, Hollis?"

"What's wrong with lying?" said Hollis. "A lie is a blow to the tyranny of fact."

"Oh, that's brilliant," said Basil. "A lie is — ? What did you just say?"

Daylight often found him in the blackest of moods. But when night fell and the wine flowed freely, none could match his flashing wit and merry gibes.

The drinks arrived on a wet plastic tray. When everyone had claimed one they lifted them silently and drank. No one said anything for a minute or two, and Rob stared in the direction of the door, toying absently with his glass.

"Isn't that one of those Linstead girls?" he said.

They all turned to look. A pair of women had just walked in; one was talking to the host and taking off her coat. The other waited for her, standing gracefully on one leg with the other leg cocked up behind her. As they watched she rummaged in her purse, took out a scrunchy, and put her long blond hair through it.

"It's Fay," said Basil. "It's not like they're twins, you know. Kay's a lot shorter."

He craned his neck for a few moments, then looked away.

"Let's not stare at them, shall we?"

Fay walked over to the bar, still arranging her hair.

"Once I was at this party at the Snail Club," Basil said. "And Kay pulled me into the bathroom with her. She just wanted to mess around a little, I guess, I don't know. Anna was there that night, and I wanted to get out without anybody seeing us together, but I couldn't figure out how, so I started to climb out the window, but I was too drunk and I ended up just falling out instead. It was only on the first floor. But guess who was in the driveway? Fay. She was on her hands and knees, throwing up, and I landed on her."

He looked over again.

"Look at her jaw. They both have these Dudley Do-Right chins."

"It's not like anybody forced you to sleep with her or anything," said Rob.

"Actually, I didn't sleep with her, if you really want to know."

"Really?" Peters leaned forward. "Is she a virgin?"

"A virgin?"

"Oh, God," said Rob. "Don't talk about it."

Basil shrugged. "She was never not so by my hand," he said.

The women sat down at the bar; Fay sat with her back to it, leaning back on her elbows, and a tall, red-faced man came over and kissed them both on the cheek.

"You never went out with her, did you, Hollis?" said Rob.

"A gentleman never tells." He took another sip of his gin and tonic.

Peters announced that he had to go to the bathroom, and Blake stood up to let him out. More drinks came. As the waiter unloaded them, mariachi music started blaring out of some lo-fi-looking speakers up near the ceiling. Hollis began to feel slightly detached from what was going on around him. He leaned back against his corner of the booth and let his head rest against the wall, while the others kept talking.

Sea marks of dark seaweed, limp searags, laid out in parallel on a bank of yellow sand. Shreds of foam arise and subside upon a field of green-and-blue swells.

I am Chingachgook—the Last of the Mohicans.

"It's not like a horse is going to be much help in a dungeon," said Blake. "It's just going to fall in a pit, or something. Step on a caltrop. Then you basically have to shoot it."

"What's a caltrop?" Basil asked.

"It's a trap. Ah — a little spiky thing."

He looked around for something to illustrate with.

"It has four points, like a pyramid. They make it so however it lands, there's always a spike pointing straight up. And it's small: you just drop a whole bunch of them on the ground if someone's chasing you on horseback, and the horse steps on them."

"Jesus Christ."

"Or in a car," said Peters. "It works on tires. They still use them, actually."

Blake sipped his martini and made a face.

"Is it bad?" Basil asked.

"Too strong."

He took another sip and shivered.

"Yeesh." He shivered again. "Too much vermouth."

"And what are you going to do with it?" said Hollis. "Even outside a dungeon. The horse, I mean. Joust? There's no point in jousting in D&D. I doubt I ever even owned a lance. All your adventuring gets done in a space that's relatively tightly circumscribed — "

Rob snorted derisively. "All *your* adventuring, maybe — "

"But it doesn't have to be a horse anyway," said Blake. "It can be anything you can ride. Like a hippogriff. Or — "

He thought hard for a second.

"Or a pseudo-dragon."

"Oh, sure," said Basil. "A pseudo-dragon. Good thinking."

"Gentlemen," said Peters, raising his glass. "Please. I give you caltrops."

They all drank.

Hollis closed his eyes and opened them again. Time seemed to be accelerating.

"Fair knight," said the Maiden, "if you would agree to tarry with me here, and leave aside your questing ways, I should be most grateful."
"That shall I not," said the Knight.
He made as if to fasten on his helm.
"Oh please, fair knight," said she, her bosom heaving. "Leave aside the ways of battle!"
"That shall I not," repeated the Knight. "For I do seek the Grail."

"First of all," he heard Blake saying, when he focused again, "there'd be no noise in space. No torpedo noises, no explosion noises. Right? If you don't have any air you can't have noises, right? There's no medium to . . . whatever. Propagate it with. The noise. No big roaring noise when the *Enterprise* goes by, or anything like that. None of those signature *Star Trek* subsonics."

His pale skin was flushed pink under his goatee. The waiter brought more drinks. Blake kept talking while he unloaded them with both hands.

"In fact" — he held up his finger — "you don't really use engines in space that much at all, really, since" — he stabbed his finger down on the table — "a ship proceeds at a constant velocity in free fall. In a vacuum. Right? There's nothing to slow it down."

He took a sip.

"Microparticles," said Rob. "Maybe. Actually, they can carry sound, too — "

"It just keeps going by itself. You only use engines when you accelerate or decelerate. None of this fucking 'She can't take much more o' this, Cap'n!' It's space, right? You just coast, all the way!"

"That's it, Blake," said Peters. "Get angry."

"Well, but think about it," said Hollis. "What do we really know about warp anyway? They might be right."

He sat back against the back of the booth. He hadn't said any-thing for a while, and suddenly everybody was looking at him.

"What if warp is more like water? Maybe you *need* to run the engine all the time, just like a ship needs its propeller going all the time, to fight against the resistance of the water. See what I'm saying? Maybe there's resistance, and you have to keep pushing all the time, or you just slow down and stop. What if warp isn't all just coasting along all the time?"

The calculating capacity of my artificial positronic brain is approxi-mately seven trillion times that of your human brain.

"Maybe," said Blake. "Maybe. Still, they talk the same way about impulse power, too."

He thought for a moment.

"All that bridge protocol comes from nineteenth-century naval stuff, you know. It's all in Patrick O'Brian."

Tonga climbed into his skiff and paddled out into the middle of the bay. No one saw him.

"Transporters, though, that's another thing: Scotty was trapped in a transporter for eighty years, right? In the Dyson Sphere episode. He doesn't age, because he's trapped in a transporter beam. Or does he? What about Lieutenant Barclay — when *he's* stuck in the transporter, something bites him on the arm. The Transporter Psychosis episode. It's not like he's frozen in time, he's still conscious. So why doesn't Scotty age when he's trapped in the transporter beam?"

Blake finished his drink. Nobody said anything.

"Well, anyway," he said. "Think about it."

"Geordie says it's on a special diagnostic circuit."

"Your mother's on a fucking diagnostic circuit," said Peters.

A crowd of three or four people banged in through the door, talking loudly. Cold air washed through the room. More drinks arrived.

"Plus," said Blake, "if he was trapped for eighty years inside a transporter he'd go insane, even if he didn't die of old age."

"Maybe he was lying," said Peters.

"Lie is a blow to the tyranny of fact," said Hollis.

He studied the backs of his hands, wiggling his fingers.

"I think lies are good," he said. "People should lie more. Lies are like these little peepholes into a better world."

"Milord waxes eloquent," said Peters. "God, you're a cheap date, Hollis."

None could match his merry gibes.

"I heard about this perfect job the other day," said Rob. "Some of my radio friends. There's this Japanese news program that needs an entertainment reporter to cover, like, the whole U.S. scene. It has some dorky Japanese name, like *Eyepopper News* or something — you have to be fluent in Japanese. But if you were, you'd be set." He shook his head, looking a little glassy-eyed. "The money was unbelievable."

Hollis unobtrusively took his wallet out of his pocket, under the table, and counted the money in it. His hands were shaking.

Even those who tried to draw closer to him, lured by his wealth or the secret of his success

No one spoke, and Hollis's attention wandered to the rest of the bar. Warm, humid air had steamed up the windows. A woman with short dyed-blond hair sat by herself, occasionally drinking beer from a glass, with a vacant expression. She was pretty, in a schoolgirlish way. Hollis caught her eye. She looked, then looked away. Some waiters and waitresses were sitting together in a closed-off section, sipping water and talking sedately among themselves. A few had already changed into their street clothes.

"If there's a bright side to the galaxy," said Peters, more or less aimlessly, "we're on the planet that's farthest from it."

For the first time that night Hollis noticed some long strings of garlics and dried peppers that were hanging from the ceiling. He was definitely feeling the gin and tonics, and he closed his eyes and pressed on his eyelids with the tips of his fingers.

The spins started.

> There once was a man named McGee
> Who lived almost entirely on tea
> When they said, "You'll get fat."
> He replied, "What of that?"
> That insalubrious old man from

"There's a monster GSAS party tonight," said Blake. "Free beer. It's over in Lehman Hall."

"Can you get us in?" said Basil.

He shrugged.

"It'd be dicey. The Law School isn't a graduate school, strictly speaking, it's professional."

"Wise man," said Hollis. "Learn a profession."

"Forget it," said Peters. "It's too late. By God, we'll stand here, and we'll die here."

"You think she's seen me?" said Basil, fingering a button on his pinstriped vest.

"Who?" Peters asked.

"Fay."

He gestured at the bar with his chin. They looked, but she

wasn't there anymore. They found her sitting at a table with her woman friend in another part of the restaurant. The man she'd been talking to was gone.

"Signs would point to no," said Hollis.

A waiter came over to announce last call, and he gave them the check.

"My cousin's coming to stay with me tomorrow," said Rob. "He went to MIT. He stayed around here for a little while after he graduated, but he couldn't get a job — it was weird. He just lived off some kind of trust fund, till it ran out."

A glass fell and smashed behind the bar, and everybody in the room stopped talking for a second.

"After that," Rob went on, "I remember he started buying these surplus bulk food consignments because they were cheaper: crates of yams and stuff like that. Star melons. The weirdest possible stuff — all these Southeast Asian vegetables nobody'd ever even heard of. He used to go down to the docks to find them. Our whole family was just totally baffled.

Tonga stayed awake until his parents were asleep, then slipped out the window and down to the docks where the fishing boats were kept.

After a while he moved out to some town in upstate New York, with some friends of his from school. I guess it was cheaper. Now he spends all his time playing role-playing games — last I heard he was running a play-by-mail simulation of the Napoleonic Wars. In real time."

As for that, mon vieux—je n'en ai rien.

"Look," said Blake. He was carefully folding up a dollar bill into sections. He held it up. "It says, 'Tits of America'!"

Hollis picked up a salt shaker and poured out some salt onto the table. He started pushing it into a crack in the tabletop with a steak knife. Somewhere somebody was making a tone by running a finger around the rim of a wineglass.

He glanced down at his watch. Peters noticed and leaned over to him.

"*Don't fall asleep,*" he whispered.

"That's when they get you!" he shouted. "When you sleep!"

Blake slid out of the booth, followed by Peters, who heaved himself out and staggered a few steps away. The café was mostly empty, except for a few people at the bar.

"Jesus!" said Peters, stretching. "I feel like I have polio."

They worked out the money and started getting ready to go. Rob had his coat on already. He poured what was left of all their drinks into one single glass, which was already cloudy with the dregs of Basil's margarita.

He held it up, saying solemnly:

"I have created life."

They threaded their way single file through the tables and out the door. Hollis's ears rang in the sudden quietness as he put on his scarf and gloves. A dark figure on a ten-speed bicycle flew by in the darkness, gears ticking, bundled up against the cold. A half-full moon shone in the clear black sky. They stood around for a minute, just taking in deep lungfuls of the clean night air.

"I've been turning into kind of a pedophile lately," said Peters. "It's pretty disgusting. I have a real thing for that girl in *Jurassic Park*. Lex. She can't be more than fifteen."

"Are you kidding?" said Blake. He belched. "Relax, I'm sure she's like thirty-five by now."

"But not only that, there's this commercial for some local restaurant, on cable, where these two girls are talking to their mom, and —"

"Oh God," said Rob. "Don't tell me."

They stood in a loose circle at the mouth of the alley. The whole other side of the street was taken up by an Express/Structure franchise, with a row of flags of no particular nationality hanging over the entrance, shifting listlessly in a barely perceptible wind. Somewhere in the distance a car alarm was going off.

"A Man, a Plan, a Bacchanal: Anomie," said Peters, grandly.

"So Rob," said Blake. "These guys" — he pointed at Hollis and Peters — "are going to go do a crime."

"Now you've done it," said Peters. "Now we're going to have to kill them."

"We're going to go hang out in these people's house, while they're away. Peters knows them. It's no big deal, really. We're going now to pick up the key."

"Wow," said Rob. "Bum rush all those complacent homeowners."

Peters, Blake, and Basil started gravitating together in the direction of Blake's car. Rob wandered off in the general direction of Harvard Yard.

It was the last time I was to see him alive.

"Well, I'll pick you up at four, anyway," said Peters. "In two hours."

He pointed at Hollis. He was wearing black leather gloves.

"Why don't you just come with us in my car, dude?" Basil called back to Hollis. "We have room."

"I don't think so," said Hollis.

Sometimes, towards evening, a lone figure would appear on the ancient battlements. He would stand there, gazing out at the horizon. Even at that distance she could distinguish the fine cut of his robe, the glint of orange sunlight on burnished mail.

"Father, who is that man?" she asked one day.

"Some say he is the Prince of Aquitania," the old man replied. "He was banished to the ruined tower, long long ago, by order of the Emperor himself."

"Perhaps someday I shall go and visit him," she said.

"I think not, my dear," said her father gently. "Come inside now—it grows late."

Perhaps we will fall in love, she added silently, to herself. And marry!

CHAPTER 4

FRIDAY, 1:50 A.M.

Hollis walked slowly back down the alleyway, stumbling when the pavement switched from asphalt to the slippery rounded cobblestones. He was a little drunk. When he turned his head, everything bright left a faint contrail after it: the moon, the streetlights, cars up ahead of him, reflections off puddles.

Glancing up at the apartment windows that overlooked the alley, he accidentally kicked over a box of empty bottles in the gutter. They were champagne bottles, expensive ones — Moët & Chandon — and he could just make out the green of the thick, dark glass in the semidarkness. He double-checked to make sure they were all empty: they were. He kicked the box again, and one of the bottles ripped free of the damp cardboard, rattling away over the cobblestones for a few yards before it suddenly shattered.

The container can no longer contain the thing contained.

A man's voice yelled something down at him that he didn't understand.

Except for a couple of black taxi drivers leaning against an orange-and-white cab pulled up against the curb, the street was deserted. They were talking in a dialect that sounded something like Creole. Otherwise the night was quiet, and Hollis could hear the tiny whirring, switching noises the traffic lights made as they changed from green to orange to red.

He crossed. In the middle of the street a car horn honked, right behind him, and he leaped onto the sidewalk and spun around. The car was moving so fast the Doppler effect distorted the sound of the horn as it swept past him.

He watched it go. The brake lights flared as it rounded a corner, and arms waved at him out the windows on both sides. It was Basil's car.

I will kill him.

Yet stay. The enemy of my enemy is my friend.

Hollis decided to stop and deposit his check in the extra minutes before his bus came. The ATM machine was housed in a tiny enclosed storefront with a picture window, too small to be a store. The window lit up the sidewalk with a swath of white fluorescent light.

Standing outside, Hollis went through his wallet for his bank card, making a face at the brightness. Before he finished the lock clicked open, by itself.

The door swung open, just an inch. He looked up.

A woman sat perched on the plastic counter beside the ATM, next to the stacks of deposit envelopes. From where she sat she was holding the door open for Hollis with her foot. She wore black leather boots that hugged her calves, with lots of complicated lacings running up them.

Hollis opened the door and stepped inside. She withdrew her leg and folded it back under her. Her stockings were black. Inside the tiny space it was bright: fluorescent lights buzzed overhead. Crumpled-up receipts with faint purple printing on them lay all over the nubbly rubber floor.

"Thanks," said Hollis.

The woman glanced up at him for a second.

Hollis guessed she might be in her early twenties. Her longish hair was dyed a mixture of dark red and black, and it was a little lank. She wore a short velvet skirt, very dark red, and what looked like a black silk slip with a tight-fitting black leather jacket. A long string of fake-looking pearls hung around her neck. She had pale skin and a large, wide mouth. Her lipstick was a dark shade of reddish brown.

She was talking, but she wasn't speaking English. Hollis didn't recognize the language — it sounded Slavic.

It took him a second to realize that she wasn't talking on a pay phone; she was talking on the ATM's emergency help phone. A sign under it read: IN CASE OF DIFFICULTY, LIFT HANDSET. Hollis tried to eavesdrop, but all he understood was a couple of names.

When he was done with the cash machine, he put off getting his card back. He toyed absently with the bumps of the Braille instructions on their embossed metal plaque. After another minute the woman said what sounded like goodbye, and since he was standing at the machine, she handed him the phone. He hung it up.

"I can't believe you can still do that," she said matter-of-factly.

She had a big black leather handbag, and she rummaged around in it and got out some lipstick. She started putting it on in a businesslike way, using her reflection in the window.

"Do what?" said Hollis.

"Use that phone."

"Use it for what?"

"Long-distance calls," she said. She pursed her lips in the window. "You don't have to pay."

The ATM returned Hollis's card, and he took it and stepped backwards until he could lean back against the outside window.

"You don't have to pay?" he said.

"Nope."

She made an odd clicking noise with her tongue.

"Who gets the bill? The bank?"

"As far as I know."

"How does it work?"

Before she answered, the woman gave Hollis a long, very neutral look. It was startlingly pretty.

"It's a long story," she said, finally.

"That's my favorite kind."

The alcohol was making Hollis calmer than he normally would have been. Still watching him, she felt around blindly in her bag with one hand.

"Why do you want to know?" she said.

"I don't know," said Hollis. "It's just a sweet hack, I guess. A loophole. Hey — everybody wants to *épater les bourgeois*."

Them crazy French.

She came up with a lighter and a pack of Merits. In one impressively quick motion she drew out a cigarette, lit it, and dropped the lighter and the pack back in. Then she took a long drag, held it, and let it back out in a sigh.

"I thought you were going to pull a gun on me," Hollis said.

"Let's hope your luck holds."

She took another drag and held it.

"I'm only doing this out of a desire to harass corporate America," she said finally, exhaling. She gestured to him. "Pick up the phone."

Hollis picked it up. There was no dial tone: she was holding down the hang-up switch.

"When I let go of this hook," she said evenly, "the phone's going to try to dial into the customer service center. It's preset to do that. You have to stop it from doing that by dialing first. But you can't, because there's no buttons on the phone to dial with."

She watched Hollis carefully, to see if he was following, and he nodded with the phone still held up to his ear. A police car went by outside with its siren on.

"The way you dial a phone like this," she went on, "is by hitting the switch: you hit it as many times as the number you want to dial. That's basically how a rotary phone works. The trick is to do it before the phone can do its own preset dialing. So what you have to do is pick up" — she let go of the receiver — "and as fast as you can you start smacking the receiver."

She tapped on it smartly, six times in a row. When she stopped, there was silence on the line, and she looked up at Hollis expectantly. The tips of her ears stuck out from under her hair, giving her a slightly elfin look.

"Who do you want to call?" she said.

"I don't really know."

"Might as well go transcontinental. It's BayBank's nickel."

Hollis scratched his chin.

"It doesn't matter," he said. "Dial anything."

She rolled her eyes at him, then went ahead and dialed. It took her about half a minute to get six more numbers tapped in.

Hollis waited. The phone rang a few times, and an answering machine picked up.

He listened to the message, then hung up at the beep.

"Who was that?" he said.

"Me," said the woman. She made the clicking noise with her tongue again. "Do I have any messages?"

"I don't think so. Which one are you — Alix or Xanthe?"

"Guess," she said lightly.

Hollis thought for a second before he answered.

"Xanthe."

"Nope," she said. She slipped down off the plastic bench. "I only wish."

She straightened her skirt and slung her bag over her shoulder. Glancing at him once, ambivalently, she headed out the door. She wasn't walking particularly quickly, and Hollis shoved his hands in his coat pockets and followed her out into the cold. It was definitely below freezing, but she let her jacket hang open.

"What kind of a name is Xanthe?" he said.

"I don't know. It's from some poem, I think."

She turned left, the opposite way from Hollis's bus stop, but he went with her.

"Is she a good roommate?"

"She's quiet."

Then she added, as if she were ticking off the points on her fingers:

"She's obsessively neat. She sleeps exactly eleven hours a day, from nine every night to eight every morning. She can't stand noise. She has good skin. She has bad hair. And she writes poems. Oh, and she's rich, dahling, she's terribly, terribly rich."

"How are the poems?"

"I never read them."

"Maybe you could introduce me."

"I don't think you're her type."

A late-night roller-blader overtook them from behind, then skated away ahead of them, the reflective patches on his elbows slowly fading away into the darkness.

"Why not?" said Hollis.

"Well, your overcoat, for starters," she said. "That's enough right there. She'd never go for that. And she likes her men taller."

"I'm pretty tall," he said.

"But she likes them taller."

She skipped her hand lightly along the roof of a parked car, a cheap green Subaru.

"I used to have this exact car."

Hollis looked back at it for a second as they went past.

"What's wrong with my coat?" he said.

She didn't answer.

She was still walking slowly, swinging the hand with the cigarette. They were headed away from Harvard Square in the direction of Boston, up Mass Ave.; most of the stores were still very upscale — gourmet foods, futon outlets, software, a Crate & Barrel — but they got less and less chic the farther they went. In the doorway of an office building two homeless people sat under army blankets. One of them asked her for a cigarette as they went by.

She shook her head, without looking: "Sorry."

A cold wind blew down the wide street and gusted in their faces.

"Where'd you learn that phone trick?" Hollis asked.

"From a book," she said. "I have this friend in Stockholm, who I call sometimes. It started adding up after a while, and I needed a way to cut some corners."

"You're not into e-mail?"

"We're not exactly dealing with Phiber Optik on the other end. And foreign character sets can get pretty ugly when you're crossing national borders. And anyway, where's the glamour in e-mail?"

"Good question," said Hollis. "I was in Stockholm once. I got sick there, and nobody could figure out what it was. I went to the emergency room, and it turned out I had scurvy. I was back-packing around Europe and I just wasn't getting any citrus. It took them forever to figure out how to translate it."

Alix looked at him and made a face. "That's disgusting."

"I guess." Hollis shrugged. "At the time I thought it was glam-orous."

She snorted. "It's a fine line."

"I thought that stuff was extinct, anyway," he said. "I had to live on limes for like, six weeks." Hollis kicked a pebble along the street with his boot. "So aren't you afraid the bank's going to catch you?"

"In a way, I'm surprised it hasn't happened yet."

Across the street, a policeman idly rapped on a parking meter with his nightstick, and she raised her voice as they passed him:

"I'm surprised they haven't caught me yet!

"I try to call at different times. So far that's been good enough."

"You know there's a camera in there."

"I know there's a camera in there," she said sharply. "Not being a complete idiot."

She flicked her cigarette down into the grate of a storm drain. It sparked redly in the darkness before disappearing into the depths.

"What do you think I was doing sitting up there on that stupid shelf? I'm pretty sure there's a blind spot there, where the cam-eras can't reach. I doubt they monitor twenty-four hours anyway. And who do you think they were looking at the whole time I was on the phone, camera-boy? You, that's who."

Hollis was silent for a few seconds.

"Well, I always wanted to be on TV," he said finally.

His resources of indifference were immense

They walked together as far as Central Square, a broad, complicated intersection where the residential neighborhoods of Cambridge started to give way to the poorer, more industrial zone of Cambridgeport. It was a bad area, and even this late at night there was a lot of activity: cops, homeless people, prostitutes, hostile young men, white, black, and Hispanic, all milling around aimlessly. The only stores open were a Rite Aid and a Dunkin' Donuts that did its business through a window in a metal shutter. Every possible surface — lampposts, bus shelters, construction sites, the stairs down to the subway — was covered with cheap paper fliers. One of the buildings on the square was burned out and sagging in on itself.

A little past the square an enormous old brick warehouse took up an entire block. It had the words STORAGE WAREHOUSE: FIRE-PROOF painted along one blind wall in gigantic white letters fifteen feet high; someone had blackened out the first few to make it read, RAGE WAREHOUSE: IREPROOF. Except for a few irregularities in the upper stories, it was built in the shape of a perfect cube. Naked orange security spotlights were bolted to the outer walls. Alix turned in at the side street before it and walked as far as the warehouse's front entrance, a cement loading dock with massive metal double doors painted battleship gray, where she stopped. Set in one of the big doors, like a pass door in a portcullis, was a smaller door with a regular brass doorknob.

Hollis looked around in the sky for the moon, but he couldn't find it, even though the sky was clear. Either it hadn't risen yet or it was blocked by the brick bulk of the warehouse. Somewhere off in the distance, in an indeterminate direction, somebody was doggedly improvising jazz, unaccompanied, on a tinny old piano.

Alix clicked her tongue again.

"What's that noise you keep making?" said Hollis.

Instead of answering, she stuck her tongue out at him for a second, and he caught a glimpse of silver metal.

"I got it done a few weeks ago," she said. "The swelling just went down. Do you have any? Pierces, I mean?"

He shook his head. Now that he noticed, she had a tiny silver ring in her eyebrow, too.

"Maybe when I get some cash," he said. "At this point I can barely keep my hair blond."

"How come you don't have any cash?"

"I don't know," said Hollis. "I get that one a lot."

They stood facing each other, in the pinkish light of the loading dock.

"So this is where you live?" said Hollis.

"Sure is."

"I didn't even know they even had apartments in here."

"Ours is the only one."

She stood with her hands on her hips, but she wasn't looking at him; she was looking off into the darkness. It wasn't quite as cold as it was before — they were out of the direct force of the wind. A pair of motorcycles went by on Mass Ave, and the noise from the pipes was so loud they had to wait a few seconds before either of them could say anything.

Finally, Alix went over to the small door that was set in the larger one.

"Watch," she said. She showed him her empty hand, palm open, both sides. Then she held it up in front of the door, where a doorbell would have been.

"Nothing up my sleeves."

A little green LED on the doorjamb lit up, and the lock buzzed open.

She held the door for him, and he stepped through.

"Pay no attention to the man behind the curtain," said Hollis.

Inside it was completely dark except for a glowing dot in the distance. As he came closer it turned out to be an elevator button down at the far end of a corridor. Alix pushed him down the hall ahead of her, with her hand between his shoulder blades.

"It's like that scene in *Diva*," he said. "The elevator shaft is empty, and I plummet down it to my death."

"A little trust, please."

She hit the button, and far away above them in the building Hollis heard and felt old, heavy machinery engaging. The darkness in the hallway was total: he closed his eyes, and there was no change at all. It was both disorienting and comforting at the same time. He leaned back against the cinder-block wall behind him; the coolness felt good against the back of his head. He felt almost sober now: the drinks had left him with nothing except a slightly dissociated feeling.

Alix stood somewhere nearby to his left. He guessed she was standing in front of the elevator doors, and he took a step forward, reaching out blindly, but there was nobody there. He stopped short and flailed his arms for a second to keep his balance. Taking another step away from the safety of the wall, he put his arms out on either side of him, and stretched, but he couldn't find her.

Quickly, Igor—the monster has escaped!

Suddenly the elevator doors opened, and the whole scene was lit up with fluorescent light. Alix was standing a few yards away, picking intently at her black-painted nails.

They stepped into the elevator together, and she took out a

tube key on a leather thong that was hanging around her neck. She fitted it into a round keyhole on the control panel, turned it, and hit the button for the top floor.

The elevator took them down, down, far below the devastation on the surface, down through endless strata of soil and rock. He felt his ears pop from the pressure change. The air smelled of cordite.

A diagram on the monitor showed them approaching the lower limits of the terrestrial lithosphere, and a warning alarm began to sound. Suddenly she was in his arms, pressing her soft, slender form up against him.

"Together, we will start the human race anew," she whispered in his ear. "Tonight—"

It was an old-fashioned freight elevator, with metal bars instead of walls. The floors they passed on their way up were marked with messily hand-painted numbers, as if someone had done them from the elevator while it was still moving.

"Quite the gilded little cage you have here," said Hollis.

"Wait till you see the apartment," she said wryly. "The buildup is better than the payoff."

When they reached the top, Alix hauled the heavy door to one side with a metallic crash. It was a short, dirty white hallway with a single door at the far end. The door had a whole column of locks and latches on it, extending above and below the door handle, and she went down them in order, undoing each one with a different key.

"I wanted to put in some kind of a pass-card system," she whispered. "The landlord wasn't into it."

The door was like the door of a bank vault, and it swung open on big, reinforced metal hinges. On the other side was a long, narrow room, startlingly tall, like the nave of a miniature cathe-

dral. A faint trace of muted, sepia-colored light came from a
heavily shaded floor lamp in a corner. The floor and the walls
were covered with layers of oriental rugs. Alix went ahead of
him, moving quickly and silently through the room to a door in
the far wall. She looked back at Hollis and put a finger up to her
lips, pointing at an overstuffed couch with her other hand: a
woman was sleeping there, curled up under a heap of blankets,
her long brown hair falling over her face.

They slipped past her and through a kitchen, into another
bedroom. Its brick walls were covered with hundreds of wooden
cubbyholes, mostly full of books — the rest of the brick was plas-
tered with photographs and posters. A giant-sized portrait of
Tintin and Snowy in bright primary colors hung suspended over
the bed, like a banner at a political rally. The ceiling gave way to
a skylight, and someone had managed to hang a couple of strings
of white Christmas lights from it, like stars.

There were two small square windows that looked like they
didn't open. Hollis started walking over to the nearer one, but an
artsy black-and-white photograph caught his attention: it was a
contact print of a woman sitting very straight and upright on
what looked like a leather psychoanalyst's couch. She was naked
from the waist up, and she was cupping one of her smallish
breasts in one hand. The other breast was bare. Hollis bent down
to look at it. The woman's hair fell over her face; he couldn't decide whether or not it was Alix.

The door closed behind him. She came in from the kitchen.

"Do you want something to drink?" she said. "Or should I say,
something more to drink? I think I have some Scotch."

"Thanks. That would be nice."

She took a bottle and two shot glasses down from one of the
cubbyholes.

"This place used to be a factory. They made bomb casings

here in World War One. That's what these little compartments are for. They stored the bombs in them."

"Handy."

She passed Hollis a glass with a generous double shot in it, and they drank together. Then she sank down into an overstuffed armchair, which rocked backwards on springs under her weight.

"In a way, I can't believe you let me in here," said Hollis, watching her.

She shrugged. "If one of us is a criminal mastermind here, it's probably me. You don't much strike me as the evildoer type. I see evildoers as more the self-starter type of person. Anyway, where's your spandex costume?"

"Maybe you caught me on dress-down day."

Don't quit your day job.

She took another sip of the Scotch.

"Do you go to Harvard?" she said.

Hollis nodded. "I used to."

"What did you major in?"

"Urban Studies."

She grimaced. "What the hell is that?"

"I forget exactly," he said. "I think there was a large filmic component."

Hollis glanced out one of the windows. Through the thick plastic he could see down into a lot behind the warehouse, partitioned off by a chain-link fence. A massive explosion of green weeds had survived the chill of fall. Then he turned away and sat down on the edge of the bed, and a ginger-and-white cat zipped out from under it, its legs twinkling.

A witch and her familiar.

"That's a mighty big rig you're driving," Hollis said, and he nodded at her computer, which was set up on its own on a long table against one wall. It had a massive megapixel monitor the size of an air conditioner. A standard rainbow-colored screen saver was running. Cables from half a dozen peripherals ran out from behind it onto the floor, all twining together down into one overgrown power strip.

"If you're going to steal something, steal that," she said. "It's worth all the rest of this stuff combined."

"Is that what you do for a living? You write code?"

"Not exactly. But it pays for some extras."

"Like what?"

"Like trips and stuff. And this place. Drugs."

Hollis laughed. "Drugs?" he said. "Do you have some?"

Her eyes narrowed a little.

"Maybe when we know each other a little better," she said.

"So I don't strike you as a criminal?" He took another slug of his whiskey. "What do I strike you as?"

Instead of answering right away, Alix got up, closed the door, and went over to the bed. She lay back on the pillows, at the other end from him.

"You strike me," she said, "as a hick who stayed out too late."

"Ouch." He made a face.

"The truth hurts."

He finished the Scotch and set the empty glass on the floor.

"Tell me something," he said. He slid up the bed and lay down next to her. "Is that you, in that picture over there?"

"Which one?"

Hollis pointed, and she propped herself up on one elbow to look.

"That black-and-white one," he said. "Next to the window."

She looked at it for a second, then at him, and then instead of answering she leaned down and kissed him on the lips, with her broad, dark mouth.

"What does it matter?" she said, after another second.

"It matters to me," said Hollis.

"Why?" She drew back a millimeter. "Do you think she's pretty?"

"I just like to know," he said.

Her nose was still cold from their walk home. She kissed him hard, without opening her mouth, and Hollis brought his hand up to her waist. He was surprised when he felt how thin her blouse was: it was just a silk slip.

When they broke apart again he whispered: "You must have been cold in just this."

She rolled over on top of him, and they kissed again, longer this time, and this time her lips were open. He put his hand up and covered her breast with his hand, and she caught her breath softly. She was very flat-chested, and she wasn't wearing a bra. He could feel her nipple against his palm.

It was surprisingly warm and quiet in the apartment. Alix's bed was a real bed, and the mattress seemed unbelievably soft and giving after his hard futon at home. He put his other hand up under her slip and let it wander up her back. She was very slender. She pushed his coat down off his shoulders, and he let go of her to wriggle his arms out of it. He could already feel lipstick getting all over his face.

The cat mewed at the door, trying to get back inside.

A long time went by. He noticed a clock ticking somewhere not far away. It took him a minute before he found it.

"Oh, God," he said suddenly. "It's after three."

"So what?" she whispered.

"I have to be somewhere." He sighed and sank back. "Soon. At four."

The clock was over the bed. It was made in the shape of a black-and-white cat, with eyes that moved back and forth to mark the seconds. The pendulum was its tail.

He sighed again and closed his eyes. The soft pillows under his head made him want to fall asleep, and he grayed out for a few seconds.

"What, you have a date?" she said.

"It's a long story."

That's my favorite kind.

"What kind of a story?"

"What kind?" He sat up and swung his legs down off the bed. He put his head down onto his hands. "I don't know. I guess you could say it's a dromedy."

She propped herself up on her elbows behind him. She was disheveled, halfway out of her slip, and looking at her Hollis felt a pulse of renewed desire.

He explained what he and Peters were doing.

"Dover?" she said when he was finished. She seemed a little unnerved. "What's in Dover? Whose house is it?"

"Just these people's. Their name is Donnelly — Peters knows them."

"Oh."

Hollis found his boots and tied the laces with big, loopy bows. When he stood up, his weight came down on the shot glass he'd been drinking out of, and it squirted out from under his boot across the hardwood floor.

"Forget about it," she said. "You can't break those things. Come on, I'll walk you out."

She pushed the strap of her slip back up and heaved herself up off the bed, giving Hollis a momentary flash of dark hair as it rode up over her white thighs. He found his coat in the bedclothes and picked it up. She led the way as they walked back along the length of the long room and through the kitchen, she pulling him along by one hand, he tagging along behind.

Her roommate was still asleep, an old T-shirt folded across her eyes. They made their way through her bedroom to the outer door.

Hollis went ahead of her out into the hall, carrying his coat. Alix stayed behind in the doorway. Her lipstick was mostly gone, and her face looked almost unfamiliar in the harsh light. He noticed for the first time that she had a small tattoo on her neck, a simple blue-green circle.

She kissed him on the cheek.

"Good night, Alix," he said.

She shook her head slowly.

"I was lying," she said. "You were right the first time. I *am* Xanthe."

Then she put her head back inside and closed the door, and Hollis stood there for a few seconds, blinking, before he turned and walked slowly back down the hall toward the elevator. It was cold on the way down, after the warmth of her apartment: the rest of the building didn't seem to be heated. He shrugged into his coat. The air smelled like wet paint.

Back outside in the street the night was quieter than before. The moon was finally visible, with a thick, cream-colored ring of refracted light around it. Hollis looked around the edge of the door for a nameplate or a mailbox, but there was absolutely nothing to show that anybody lived there. He jumped down off the loading dock and backed away from it, looking up, trying to find even a lighted window, but there was only darkness.

Quite a three-pipe problem, Watson.

It was all a dream.

A miniature maelstrom of leaves formed nearby. It wandered over to Hollis, whirling around him for a few seconds, before it dispersed into nothingness again.

After another minute he gave up and walked away down the darkened street.

CHAPTER 5

FRIDAY, 3:30 A.M.

The bus stop was opposite the one he'd gotten off at before. The street was quieter and darker now, and the marquee over the movie theater where he'd met Peters had been turned off. A few leaves lay scattered across the brick sidewalk. There was no traffic, and the little park was deserted now. A young Hispanic-looking man ran past Hollis going the other way, his hands jammed into the pockets of a satin varsity jacket.

The stop was on a corner in front of an office building, and the company that owned the building had turned the sidewalk into a little brick plaza with a greenish bronze sundial in the middle, lit up by an orange-pink streetlight. A couple sat waiting on one of the benches, both wearing black leather coats, and

Hollis recognized one of them: she worked behind the counter at a used-clothing store near his apartment in Allston. She was a tiny woman, barely five feet tall, with an almost shockingly thin waist. Her complexion was deathly pale. She wore stockings with fat horizontal Dr. Seuss stripes on them. The two talked quietly, and the man kept snapping his fingers excitedly whenever he made a point.

Nay, my brothers. She is not the one we seek.

Hollis sat down on the other bench. He didn't have to wait long: in a couple of minutes the bus appeared at the corner, its tires squeaking and grinding against the curb. The pavement sparkled in the headlights. The lights were on inside — it was almost empty. He paid and walked back to an empty row of blue plastic seats towards the middle, and the bus whined and heaved itself forward.

There were hot-air blowers in the ceiling, and Hollis shivered and opened his coat. He felt exhausted. He could see his reflection in the opposite window, looking slightly bleary-eyed. His face was getting stubbly, and his coat collar was standing up on one side. Outside, behind his reflection, shadowy buildings slid by, followed by the headlights of a car waiting at an intersection, and then the bus reached the bridge and there was a view of the Charles River: a wide expanse of dark water and white reflected light broken up into tiny wavelets. On one side was a huge Victorian boathouse that belonged to Harvard. The other side was overgrown with a dark mass of shrubbery.

Upstream Hollis could see the lights of Mt. Auburn Hospital, buried among the trees.

In 1873 the body of an unidentified young woman was recovered from the Seine River in Paris. A plaster death mask was taken of her face, and under the name L'Inconnue de la Seine *it became one of the most striking and popular icons of nineteenth-century French Romanticism.*

The woman from the clothing store got up unsteadily from where she'd been sitting, next to her boyfriend. She staggered to another seat, dropped into it, and looked back at him coyly.

"I can't sit going sideways," she said, primly crossing her legs.

There were only five or six other passengers. The change-sorting machine at the front of the bus was clacking and jingling loudly. The digits of a giant LED clock flew by outside, in front of a bank. It was a quarter of four.

The bomb is set to go off in fifteen minutes. You must stop this insanity before it goes any further.

Past the bridge Hollis saw the huge Harvard sports complex. A giant inflated tennis Quonset loomed in the distance, across a dark plain of playing fields. The bus stopped at a traffic light.

Hollis closed his eyes.

The tide had come in while they were sitting talking, and the only path back to the beach was six feet underwater. The rest of the rocky point was fenced off by a private estate. Hollis wanted to swim back across the cove, but Eileen thought it was too choppy—they'd never make it out through the surf. Neither of them could remember how long it took for the tide to go out again.

"Well, Skipper," she said, getting up from where she was sitting and dusting sand off her thighs, "I say we climb that fence and get the hell out of here."

"Hang on," said Hollis, from where he was lying. "My Spidey-sense is tingling. That means trouble."

Eileen sat down on a boulder.

The sun was only about an hour above the horizon. The sea was a dark blue. The air was cooling, but the rocks were still warm, and from where they were sitting they could see the beach and the row of summer mansions that ran along behind it, and the tiny beachgoers laid out in ragged parallel rows along the sand.

Half an hour went by.

"Okay," said Hollis finally. He sat up and stretched. "I give in."

Eileen's eyes were closed. She wriggled a little where she was lying. "I was just getting comfortable," she said. "Gimme another sec."

"You can have all the sex you want."

The bus stopped every few blocks, but no one got on or off. Hollis let his head lie back against the hard back of the seat, with his legs stretched out across the aisle. He felt the bus turn a corner and climb up a bridge which ran over an abandoned railway yard. He knew what it looked like in daylight: brown steel rails and brown wooden sleepers with weeds poking up between them. There were complicated mechanical shunting devices at the intersections, now rusted into place. A few blasted-looking old railroad cars still stood on the tracks, painted bright primary toy-colors.

Here lies the wasteland of X, where once the mighty wizard Y did battle with the mighty wizard Z

The bus turned a sharp corner, and a collection of candy wrappers and Styrofoam cups slid out from under the seats and across the floor. An oversized can of Foster's rolled after them in irregular, sloshing jerks — it was still half full.

At that moment, the futility of his existence was suddenly borne in upon him.

Hollis slid down even farther in his seat, until he could see the streetlights opposite him going by overhead, linked to one another by power lines that resembled long rising and falling swells. The sky behind them was a mist of orange and gray. The tiny woman and her boyfriend were sitting next to each other again. At the back of the bus a thin black man sat bolt upright, listening to a Walkman.

After ten minutes they were almost at Hollis's stop, and he got up and went to stand at the front of the bus for the last block. A trio of twenty-something women were getting off at the same time, tipsy secretaries having a night out.

"Please retrieve your baggage from under the seats," said one of them, giggling. "Before exiting the airplane."

I am not capable of human emotion, Doctor. I am unable to "laugh" at what you call "humor."

The whole intersection was lit up with floodlights, and a crowd was milling around noisily on the sidewalks — mostly college students from BU and BC. A few bars and clubs were still open, and a Store 24. Hollis pushed through the crowd as fast as he could. The night was quieter and darker after he got a few blocks up Commonwealth to where the residential buildings started. For some reason, the roofs were all crenellated, and silhouetted against the sky they looked like one single unbroken fortified wall. He passed a lamppost festooned with yards and yards of magnetic ribbon from an unwound cassette tape.

On May 21, 1991, while campaigning in Sriperumbudur, south of Madras, former prime minister Rajiv Gandhi was approached by a young woman wearing a loose-fitting green-and-orange robe. As the woman bowed to Mr. Gandhi in a traditional gesture of respect, she apparently detonated a bomb made of plastique mixed with steel ball bearings which she wore strapped to her body beneath her clothing. All that remained after the explosion was her head, which was found nearby almost perfectly intact.

The street in front of Hollis's building was divided by the trolley tracks, and someone had gotten stuck in one of the lanes going the wrong way. Now the driver gingerly tried to back up to where he'd made the mistake, in the glare of the headlights of the oncoming cars. A group of partygoers watched from the sidewalk.

"Now I've seen everything," said a woman's voice.

The trolley had stopped running hours earlier. He could hear the wind blowing in the trees, and there was a crisp smell of snow in the air. A plastic upright fan stood leaned up against a tree in front of his building; for some reason the trash people wouldn't collect it.

In the elevator, Hollis leaned back against the wall and took a deep breath. The door opened. He walked mechanically to his apartment and unlocked it — it took him a few tries to get both locks undone. His futon was still folded up into a couch. There were no messages on the machine.

As he unlocked his bicycle outside her apartment, he noticed he was having trouble breathing.

"I'm dead," he thought. "I'll never survive."

The square dial of the clock on his desk read 3:55. Hollis went into the bathroom and sat down on the cold tile floor, still wearing his green corduroy overcoat. The radiator hissed crazily.

One night Hollis came back to his building late. He was surprised to see a man standing in the hallway outside his apartment—it was unusual for anyone else in the building to be up at this hour. The man was dressed in a gray suit, somber but expensively cut. For some reason he struck Hollis as strangely familiar.

"Hollis Kessler," said the stranger. "Do you know who I am?"

Hollis stopped.

"I don't think so."

"I'm here to ask for your help. There isn't much time. I've come a long way to find you."

They faced each other.

"Our world is dying. Only you can save us."

For some reason the bathroom light was incredibly bright. Hollis ran some cold tap water into a glass and drank it. It tasted like old toothpaste.

My hands were unsteady, and a drop splashed onto the white linen of the tablecloth.

Same old Caulfield. When are you going to grow up?

Hollis closed his eyes.

It was very late. Lying on the bed, Hollis watched Eileen take off her jewelry. Her back was to him, but he caught glimpses of her face in the mirror.

"Nadia's mother looked like hell tonight," she said.

"She had that huge pin on her dress," said Hollis. "What was that thing, the Hope Rhinestone?"

When she was done Eileen came over and lay down on top of him, still in her evening gown, with the back unzipped down to the small of her back. They kissed.

After a while she pulled back and wrinkled her nose at him, smiling.

"You sweat like a pig," said Eileen. "Whenever you wear a suit."

"But I smell like a man."

"You smell like several men."

The sun is going down on a salt marsh. The tops of the reeds are all but drowned in seawater. A post marks the channel out to the ocean.

The flow of the tide carries a flat-bottomed skiff on the current, faster and faster, out towards the bay, faster and faster and faster and faster.

Eileen smoothed his forehead with her hand.

"There, then," she said. "There, then."

Twenty minutes later, Hollis was downstairs in the vestibule
of his apartment building. Even inside it was cold, and
he could see his breath in the air. The floor was decorated with tiny colored mosaic tiles, and littered with
red-and-white Chinese menus and thick bundles of
newsprint coupons.

It was still dark out. He sat down on the icy marble
steps and looked out through the glass door at the hotel
across the street: all the lights were out, and chintzy
white curtains hung in the windows. In the parking lot
a pair of police cars idled, their driver's-side windows
facing each other. Plumes of white exhaust from their
engines floated up into the light of the streetlights.

Pulling his coat around him, Hollis opened the door

and stepped out onto the stoop. The early-morning air was bitterly cold. He leaned back against the door. His face felt a little raw from having been hastily washed and scrubbed. A pair of headlights caught his eye as they appeared at the top of the hill. He watched them as they headed down the hill towards him. At the last possible second the car slowed down and stopped, its tires whimpering on the pavement.

It was a clean, sleek, new-looking gray Lexus sedan. Hollis could barely hear the engine running. A moth fluttered crazily in front of one of the headlights, in and out of the thick white beams.

One day, my son, all this will be yours.

Hollis jogged down the steps, between the parked cars, and out into the street. He opened the door: it was warm in the car, and Peters sat behind the wheel, staring straight ahead at the road, wearing a furry leather hunting cap with earflaps. There were dark circles under his eyes. Hollis climbed in. Neither of them said anything, and Peters eased off the brake. They rolled forward up to the stoplight at the corner.

"Pretty nice car," said Hollis, while they waited.

Peters nodded.

"Where's your hat?" he said.

"I don't have one."

"Take one." Peters gestured towards the backseat. "Have a hat. Thieves always have hats."

Hollis turned around; there was a fedora on the back seat. He made a face and turned back around again.

"My father wears those," he said.

"How is the old man, anyway?"

The light changed, and Peters stamped on the accelerator.

"Who knows?" said Hollis.

Trees, street signs, and gray stoops flew by. They passed a block of nicer buildings with identical green canopies over the doorways; in the window of each one was an identical little brass-colored chandelier.

"Did you sleep?"

"No," Peters said. "Blake and I played poker at his place."

"Did you win the car?"

"We stuck to bets I could cover."

"A deck of cards is the devil's prayerbook."

Peters nodded, yawning.

"I'm not really feeling all that verbal right now, dude," he said.

They beat three or four red lights in a row until they reached the main intersection, where Hollis had gotten off the bus half an hour earlier. The street corners were mostly empty now, and in the window of a Woolworth's Hollis could see rows of cages with parakeets in them, in various fluorescent colors, sleeping with their heads resting on their own shoulders. There was no other traffic, and when the light changed Peters pushed the Lexus up to fifty. The road widened out into eight lanes. Off to their left the Charles appeared and disappeared in the darkness between the buildings. They cut right through the BU campus, with high-rise classroom buildings on one side and rows of campus stores on the other.

Hollis leaned his seat back and closed his eyes.

IT WAS A RACE TO THE EDGE OF SPACE . . .

The ship was the size of a six-story apartment building, and not much more aerodynamic. The squared-off hull was built for interstellar flight, and in the thick lower atmosphere it was all he could do to keep its nose pointed at the sky. The gravity projectors that held it up were drawing every last watt of reserve power.

He knew he had no hope of outrunning the nimble military fighters that harried him, but there was a chance his shielding might hold out

*until they reached the ionosphere. Then the hyperdrive would kick in,
and in an instant the bulky ship would become as quick and agile as
a fish in water. It was a race to the edge of space.*

*If only, he thought, if only I knew for sure it was a race I wanted to
win. . . .*

After another five minutes Peters swung them up the on-ramp to
the westbound Massachusetts Turnpike. When the plump
middle-aged woman in the tollbooth leaned down to give Peters
his ticket, her blouse fell open a little, and even from the passenger seat Hollis got a generous look at her freckled cleavage.
She wore an ebony pendant shaped like a fish. Then they were
through, and Peters took them over to the left lane. He pushed
them up to eighty-five without the engine showing any sign of
strain.

"What are we going to do when we get there?" said Hollis
drowsily. "I mean, shouldn't we talk about it beforehand?"

"Good question," said Peters. "I don't really know."

Hollis grimaced and closed his eyes again.

There was a pretty girl on my vidphone screen.

I'd never seen her before. It was the last time I was to see her alive.

*"EEC security is chiefly dependent on the Mendel algorithm for
generating its passcodes," she was saying. "Once you have the en-
cryption chip, you'll be able to walk right in the front door."*

*She started reciting a long list of interface parameters. The vidphone
display showed a pretty oval face, with a high forehead and short
brown hair wrapped up in a scarf. The room in the background was
dark and indistinct.*

*"Your Mitsubishi-Hirsch contact will be at the gate," she went on.
"He has a tattoo, here"—she touched a place on her neck—"that will
register only with your augmented vision. Don't break stride when you
see him."*

"Wait," I said. "Wait a minute. Who are you?"

She cut me off. I realized only then that she couldn't hear me. I was talking to a recording.

"If my status at EEC has not been compromised, I may still be alive when you receive this message. Do not try to contact me. For our mutual safety, we must never meet."

The girl's eyes seemed to lock with mine, and there was a trace of pleading under the even coolness of her demeanor. She couldn't have been more than eighteen.

"Watch for the sign of the black fish."

The vidphone screen went dark.

A two-by-four lying in the road flashed in the headlights for an instant, and Peters swerved nimbly to put it between the front wheels. Hollis watched him feel around with one hand for the cigarette lighter, then look down and punch it in.

"I guess it should be me who goes in," Peters said finally. "If they catch me I'll be sort of fucked, because they know who I am, but on the other hand they probably won't call the police or anything. They'll just be a little weirded out — like, what am I doing robbing their house?"

"Good question," said Hollis.

"Even if I step in, they'd probably call the police on you. That would be a disaster."

"I can't imagine what you'd say."

"Besides, I know the house," Peters said. "It'll take five minutes. Max. You just stay in the car."

Hollis nodded and looked out the window.

"We'll never make it there by dawn," he said.

The lighter popped back out, but Peters didn't seem to notice.

The highway slowly descended towards ground level as they left the city. In the darkness, beyond the pale sand of the shoulder, a bumpy line of dark trees flew by. A wide, placid reservoir appeared, and it took almost a minute for it to slide slowly past in the moonlight. There was a tiny island in the middle, with trees that leaned out from the shore to overhang the dark water.

Our island home is far beyond the waves.

"Is it still daylight savings time now?" Hollis asked.

"Not anymore, old sport. Look for a sign that says 128. 128 or 95, they're the same thing. Jesus, it's been ages since I did this."

He reached up and angled the rearview mirror so he could look into it. Pushing back his bangs, he examined his forehead.

"I ate a whole bag of potato chips with Blake," he said. "It was disgusting."

"Are you looking for boils?"

"Boils? What are boils? Pimples." He looked again. "Jesus. I think I can see my third eye."

"At camp we used to call them fee-foos."

Hollis glanced into the backseat again. There was a Wesleyan sticker on the back window.

"Do you think Blake really owns this thing?" he said.

"I don't really know. It could be. He's no pauper, our Blake. Look at the registration, if you're insatiably curious. He ain't no pauper, and he sure ain't no prince. I of course abjure all material wealth."

Peters straightened the mirror out again, and Hollis opened the glove compartment and started looking through the sheaf of papers inside. He stopped and held up a little spiral notebook.

"Check this out," he said. "Someone's keeping track of every time they stop for gas. What their mileage was, how much they used. How much it cost. Some people just have too much energy What does a registration look like, anyway?"

"Don't worry about it, we're better off not knowing." He

looked out the window at the horizon. "I wonder what time the sun comes up."

"I dunno." Hollis closed his eyes again. "I left my almanac in my other suit."

Peters snorted. "Everybody's a comedian."

He started singing:

"There is a house in something something
They call the Rising Sun."

He cleared his throat.

"And it's been the ruin of many a man
And God, I know I'm one."

Hollis powered down the window a crack, and as they passed another off-ramp he pointed it out.

"That's my home exit," he said. "I grew up about a mile from here."

Beams of white light lanced down from somewhere above us, grow-ing a deeper and deeper red as they penetrated into the blood plasma. There was something about it that seemed achingly familiar. Even Pe-terson abandoned the helm for a minute, to watch through a forward viewport. For a while nobody spoke.

"What is it?" somebody asked finally.

"We've reached the ear," said Peterson. "We're looking out through the tympanic membrane, from the inside. That light is probably sunlight."

"Jesus God!" I said. Tears flooded my eyes. "Will we ever get out of the President's body alive? Will this fantastic voyage ever end?"

A giant flashing-arrow sign passed by on their right, mounted on a little yellow trailer in the breakdown lane. The right lane was closed off. The grass of the median strip looked pale in the darkness — sometimes there was a glimmer of water in the mid-dle where the ground was especially low, or even a stand of cattails. Where the strip widened and the opposite lane drifted farther away, whole thickets and groves of trees sprang up. A midnight-blue state trooper parked in a turnaround watched them flash past without moving.

Hollis ran his finger along a seam in the leather upholstery.

"What do you think they'd get us on?" he said. "I mean, if we got caught."

"Breaking and entering, I guess. I don't know. Criminal trespassing. General moral turpitude. Why?"

"I dunno."

Hollis glanced up at the sky through the blued-glass band at the top of the windshield and frowned.

"Maybe we can get Blake arrested, too. It's his car. He aided and abetted us."

"Sure, let's all get arrested. Hey, what happened with that girl the other night?"

"What girl?" said Hollis. "I don't know any girls."

"From Amanda's party. She had some Russky name."

"Oh. Tanya. I actually went out with her the other night," he said. "Friday night. We went out for a drink, and then we ended up sitting around in her apartment. It was sort of gothic — she has some kind of obscure wasting disease that nobody knows what it is. She has to eat this special macrobiotic herb all the time, that she grows herself. Her whole apartment is full of little trays of it."

"Sounds bucolic," said Peters. "Pastoral."

"It wasn't, though, it was a disaster." He stared out the window. "She turned out to be incredibly stupid — she started talking about Bob Mould, and what a genius he's supposed to be, and I faded out."

"You have to cut these girls some slack, Hollis — they feel like they have to say a certain amount of stuff, you know, first, so if you actually sleep together it won't just turn out to be an empty sex act."

Peters looked over at him, then back at the road.

"It's supposed to be a medium for communication, right? So there has to be something that's being communicated. They know it doesn't really matter all that much what it actually is, exactly, but you can't just *do* it: you have to say something first. It's like foreplay. Do your part. Quit being so genuine all the time. You're going to have to start dissembling a little."

He stopped and punched in the cigarette lighter again.

"If you ever want to get any."

"Maybe I don't want any," said Hollis.

"Sure you do. Everybody wants some. Maybe if you had a job you'd be more in circulation."

"I don't really want a job either," said Hollis. "To be brutally frank." He powered the window back up.

"She had nice eyes," said Peters.

"Everybody has nice eyes," said Hollis. "Eyes are nice."

A pickup truck pulled abreast of them on the right. It had brackets for carrying panes of glass, but they were empty. Peters read a green-and-white highway sign that was attached to an overpass:

"A mile to 128."

"Maybe I'll ask out my Temporary Employment Contractor," said Hollis. "She told me last week that I have a lot of 'horse sense,' quote unquote. God, they despise me there."

"I bet you make a lousy temp. Jesus, Hollis, I'm going to start getting worried about you. You know what happened to you?"

"I give up. What happened to me?"

"I just thought of this — it's the American university system. This is my new theory: the New Feudalism. You go to college and you get used to living like some kind of medieval overlord, with people waiting on you and everything, and it warps your mind. It happens to everybody. By the time you graduate you have all the personal habits of an aristocrat, and none of the money. No wonder you're dysfunctional — you're a twentieth-century office temp who's channeling for a nobleman in the British Raj."

They watched a pair of red taillights appear and disappear in the distance. The embankment was so high they were on a level with the tops of the trees beside the highway.

"Maybe," said Hollis. "Maybe I'm just too darn good for this damn, dirty world."

They stopped talking. Hollis leaned his cheek against the cold glass of the window and closed his eyes. The vibration of the car transmitted itself through his jawbone. It was almost five by the clock in the dashboard. Hollis pressed his hands between his knees. There was a ragged back issue of *The New Republic* in a pocket in the door, but it was still too dark to read.

After a while he felt the car slow and turn onto Route 95. He groped around under the seat until he found the row of buttons that would recline it all the way back. Peters asked him if he was going to sleep. He grunted. He curled his legs up onto the seat.

Something sharp in his pocket was poking his thigh, and he dug it out and put it on the dashboard: his keys.

When he opened his eyes again it was after five. The very edge of the sky had turned a glowing cornflower blue, though closer to the zenith it remained a deep black.

"Morning, buttercup," said Peters. He pointed out a huge blue-glass-and-steel hotel that was emerging from the trees at the top of a low bluff. Even from the highway they could see that the lobby was at least six or seven stories high.

"Bloody great hotel," he said. "Smack in the middle of Lynn, or whatever this fucking town is. Who the hell would *pay* to stay here?"

The facade faced east. Some of the rising blue of the sky was reflected in it, divided into rectangles by the panes of glass.

"This is America's Technology Highway," said Hollis. He cleared his throat. "*Zaibatsu* territory. That's who must use it." He sniffed. "Next step, everybody lives in corporate arcologies. Never go outside. I for one can't wait."

Suddenly Peters swerved to the right. They cut across all four lanes at sixty miles an hour.

"Jesus fucking hell!" said Hollis, grabbing onto his armrest. "What the hell are you doing?"

Peters whooped as they squealed onto the exit ramp, barely missing the grass shoulder. They decelerated around the curve and managed to come to a stop by the time the ramp ended in a T intersection with a flashing yellow light.

Suddenly it was dark and still. A miniature delta of stray gravel crackled under the wheels. A white-on-green sign on the corner showed arrows pointing both ways, to Wellesley and to Dover.

"Mr. Peabody," said Peters, "set the wayback machine."

Warp nine, Scotty.

They took the Dover road. Even in the center of town the traffic lights were still flashing yellow. The houses were huge and white, and covered with columns and widow's walks and balconies and gables.

Hollis cleared his throat.

"So where is this place, anyway?" he said.

"Not that far. A few miles. Look." He pointed to a grocery store with a sign that read FATHER & SON MARKET. "Two generations of successful capitalism."

"I just decided," said Hollis. "I'm going to go see Eileen."

"You are? Why?"

"I don't know. I just decided."

Peters frowned.

"When are you going to go see her?"

"Next couple of days, I guess."

Suddenly Hollis's palms started sweating, and he wiped them on his thighs. He yawned nervously. The trees let up for a few minutes while they passed a sumptuous golf club, wide expanses of grass gleaming with dew. Afterwards the houses resumed. A police car drove past in the other direction.

"That's one," said Peters. "There's only one more cruiser in the whole town. At least we won't have the gendarmerie to deal with."

"This had better work, you know," said Hollis.

"It'll work."

He hid his mounting misgivings behind a mask of calm, easy wit.

As they went farther the landscape got more and more rural. The roads narrowed, and the woods were dark for minutes at a time. Where the land was marshy, a thick white mist flowed across the road. At the same time, the neighborhoods became wealthier: the houses were set farther back, and the driveways tended to be semicircular loops, with two separate wrought-iron gates, instead of straight lines. There were tennis courts behind screens of trees. Once they passed a fenced-off pasture with an oval dirt track, although Hollis couldn't see any horses.

They bumped over a tiny bridge that looked like it was made out of old telephone poles. Peters remarked that the stream that ran under it eventually turned into the Charles River that ran through Boston.

It seemed to lead into the heart of an immense darkness.

Finally they turned off the main road and entered a maze of curving gray streets without street signs. Peters pointed out the mouth of the street he had grown up on. Hollis turned to look over his shoulder as they passed it.

He could make out no trace of the bygone past.

Five more minutes passed, in tense silence. Then Peters word-lessly pulled over to the side of the road and killed the engine. It was exactly half past five. He switched off the lights. They were on a wide, dove-gray street with a few sizable houses visible, partly screened by trees, with more trees behind them. The only sound was the ticking of the engine as it cooled and contracted in the early morning air.

CHAPTER 7

FRIDAY, 5:30 A.M.

"This reminds me of some movie," said Hollis.

His voice sounded weirdly loud in the silence.

"It's like a lot of movies."

"We should have talked about it more."

Peters shrugged.

"What's there to talk about, really?"

A thin layer of cloud was rolling in with the dawn. The half-light reduced the landscape around them to a composition of different shades of gray, the only color being the hint of gray-blue just above the horizon. Hollis yawned again and shivered. With the heater off, the air in the car was starting to get cold. He put his hands together and breathed into them. A pair of improbably long black skid marks stretched along the asphalt in front of them and curved away around the corner out of sight.

"All right," said Peters. "You sit in the driver's seat."

He took the keys out of the ignition and dropped them jingling into Hollis's lap.

"You can drive, if we have to leave in a hurry. Which I very much doubt will happen."

"Look, why don't I just come with you?"

Hollis opened the car door a crack, and the dome light came on.

"Whatever," said Peters.

The door opened into a dark fir tree that was sopping wet with dew, and Hollis could feel the cold branches pressing against his back through the thickness of his overcoat. Peters climbed out on the other side.

"There's really no point," he said. "It'll take like two minutes. There's just more of a chance you'll knock something over and set off a motion detector or something."

"Do they have those?" said Hollis.

"They're never on."

He slammed the door and started walking away down the street, backwards.

"They're probably just a pain in the ass. Look, do you *want* to come?"

"Sort of."

"It's just that there isn't really any point."

Hollis shrugged and looked around, not moving. The street was so wide it could have been divided into four lanes, but the town had left it blank. The lawns on either side flowed into one another with no dividing lines, the property lines marked only by a hedge, or a row of trees, or a difference in the color or height of the grass.

"Well, lock the car, anyway."

Hollis jogged around to the driver's-side door and locked it, and together they walked up to the corner. As they turned onto the next street they could see only two houses. The first was a grand Victorian farmhouse with a two-tiered veranda, paired with an even larger barn. It had a folly gazebo on the land behind it, and farther back they could see a swimming pool with a high green chain-link fence around it.

They walked in the middle of the road. A crow cawed.

"Which one is it?" said Hollis.

Peters pointed to the house on the left, farther along. It was newer and even bigger than the farmhouse: Colonial, three stories tall, painted white, with a row of classical columns along the front. It was set back a few hundred feet from the road, and from where Hollis was standing he could see that it had two wings that extended back as far again as it was wide. The windows were arranged in long, regular rows, with black shutters. Five or six red brick chimneys stuck up from the gray roof at irregular intervals.

Next to the driveway, where it approached the front of the house, stood a little wrought-iron lamppost with a globular white light on top of it. The light was on.

Fair friends, here is a great marvel, for I seem to see a tree of iron.

Peters slowed his pace as they came up to the lawn, then stopped when he reached the edge. Wide stripes of ever-so-slightly lighter and darker green ran across it, left behind by a lawnmower.

"So," said Peters, in his regular speaking voice. "Somebody here order a pizza?"

"Where's the door? Around back?"

Peters nodded. "Yeah. Sure."

He stared off into the backyard, squinting. A big black bird rose up out of the trees, clapping its wings together, and flew away over their heads.

"I guess if we see anybody we can say we were cutting through," Peters said. "I don't really know what's back there. So I'm not sure exactly what we'd be cutting through to."

He stopped and shook his head. Jerking his shirt front down to smooth it out, he stepped decisively onto the grass. Hollis followed him.

They cut across the property diagonally. Dew from the grass seeped into their sneakers, and a thin white mist hung in the air a few feet above the turf. For an instant Hollis glimpsed his own face reflected in the dark windows of the first floor. As they came around the back the house turned out to be shaped like a U, with the two rear wings connected by an arched colonnade that closed off the fourth side, defining a small courtyard in the middle. A few hundred feet farther back, in the trees behind the backyard, it was still pitch dark.

Peters pointed out a little landing against the rear of the house, at the base of one of the wings. Hollis watched as he climbed up the two wooden steps. There was a metal screen door, and Peters put his hand on the handle and swung it open in slow motion. A rusty metal spring twanged as it stretched.

Behind the screen door was a wooden one, with a little cut-glass window set in it at eye level.

"Jeez, man," whispered Hollis.

"Now must to be velly kefful," said Peters softly.

He rubbed his hands together briskly and reached out for the brass knob. Glancing back at Hollis over his shoulder, he pushed in without turning. The door opened.

Danger, Will Robinson! Danger!

Hollis followed Peters in, wiping his feet on a mat on the floor as he crossed the threshold. He closed the door behind him, and suddenly it was dark. The room was a storeroom, a kind of pantry, with shelves along the walls crammed with canned goods. There was a bundle of snow shovels standing in one corner, and a huge humming white freezer against one wall. Bales of faded old *New York Times Magazines* tied with twine were piled up around it.

When they opened the door on the opposite wall, warm air puffed out around the edges. It had been sealed with weather stripping, and there was a difference in air pressure.

They stepped carefully into a silent, shining, immaculate kitchen.

For a few seconds neither of them said anything, then Hollis closed the door softly behind them.

"Welcome to the cyberbs," he whispered.

Rows and rows of copper-bottomed pots of various shapes and sizes hung on the walls. Peters walked softly across the yellow linoleum floor to a cabinet and opened a drawer. Hollis strolled after him. He opened the fridge: it was crammed. There was a six-pack of Rolling Rock on one of the bottom shelves, pine-green cans, and he detached one.

"Nice going," said Peters. "Like they won't notice."

Hollis looked at the beer in his hand.

"The die is cast," he said, and he took out the rest of the beer. He left it standing on the butcher's-block counter.

"We can drink it on the way back."

It was 5:44 in the morning, according to the green LED clock in the microwave. They moved on through an open archway into a long, hushed dining room with a huge dark-wood table in it. All the curtains were drawn, and an unearthly white light fil-

tered in through them. An enormous mirror with a heavy gilt
frame hung on the wall.

Hollis looked at himself in it.

Peephole to a better world.

Peters came up behind him.

"What do you think?" said Hollis. "Should I shave my head?"

"Grow it out," said Peters. "Grow it out. All the cool kids are
doing it."

"What about Michael Stipe?"

Peters snorted. "Like I said."

They went on into the entrance hall, which was decorated
with oriental rugs and British-looking paintings of hunting
scenes. A grandfather clock stood in one corner, its pendulum
frozen. Hollis watched impassively, drinking his beer, as Peters
went through a closet full of umbrellas and overcoats, whisper-
ing nervously to himself under his breath.

"Where's her fucking purse? Come on, you mother. Where
the fuck are you?"

The entrance hall had a grand staircase up to the second floor.
Glancing down, Hollis noticed that his feet were leaving dark im-
pressions in the white carpet. He hoped the Donnellys wouldn't
notice. It was chilly; the thermostat was turned down for the
night.

*It was an ice planet. Everything was covered over with deep, powdery
snowdrifts.*

A little light crept in through a few glass rectangles in the front
door, and Hollis could see the dawn creeping up. There were two
or three framed family photographs, which he avoided looking at.

"All right," Peters whispered, closing the sliding door of the closet. "That was a bust."

He opened it again a crack, to where it had been before.

"Look around for a purse or something," he said. "Drawers. Little hooks for hanging keys on. If it turns out it's in their bedroom, we're fucked."

They went into a kind of parlor, a long, meticulously neat room divided into two halves: at the far end was a white baby grand piano, cluttered with sheet music.

Peters looked around alertly.

"They're not going to be in here," said Hollis.

"Never say never, my dear Watson." He picked up some of the magazines and looked under them. "You see — but you do not observe."

Hollis walked over to the piano, but the keyboard was closed and locked. He buffed away a fingerprint with his sleeve.

"I'd like to send this next number out to our audience upstairs," he said. "I hope they're listening. It's called 'You Made Me Love You.'"

Peters headed through the door at the far end, and Hollis trotted after him. They emerged in a short hallway with an elaborate red velvet window seat. Several corridors fanned out from it. The window looked out onto a few hundred feet of lawn and the next house down the street. It was still too early to see colors.

Somehow the view was oppressive to me, and I rang for the curtains to be closed.

"Jesus, Hollis," said Peters. "Are you even paying attention?"

"Sorry." He turned away from the window. "What's next, boss?"

"We split up. You do that part" — he pointed down another

corridor — "I'll go around the other way and meet you back at the stairs. In five minutes."

"Back in a flash," said Hollis. "Without the cash."

When Peters was gone, Hollis turned and walked slowly down the hall he'd pointed at. Without Peters the house was suddenly quiet. He started opening doors: a guest bathroom, a closet full of linens and old hotel soap, and a door that opened back onto the living room with the piano.

The last door was a tall archway that led into a second, less formal dining room, surprisingly bright and airy. In the middle was a glass-topped table with a porcelain vase full of dried flowers, sitting on a doily. A pair of French doors looked out onto the courtyard; incongruously, they were chained and padlocked shut.

Hollis pulled out a chair and sat down at the table. The early-morning light reflected off the glass, and he could see traces where someone had wiped the table with a washcloth and left it to dry.

Millions of years ago the Eastern Seaboard region of the North American continent was entirely underwater, from as far north as Boston to as far south as Atlanta.

Hollis slouched down in the chrome-and-wicker chair. There were some framed Audubon bird drawings on the wall facing him. What he could see of the courtyard outside was a plain green lawn, with a curious four-cornered fountain made of some kind of patinated metal in the center. At each of the four corners was perched a little cherub, struggling to hold on to a fish that might in warmer weather have been spouting water.

He felt tired. Time was passing.

They were sitting together in the library. It was winter, and somebody was sweeping snow off the roof over their heads. They could hear the

*clumping sound of his boots through the ceiling, and with every push
of the pushbroom a whole snowbank drifted down past the window, lit
up in the bright winter sunlight, in a regular rhythm. Inside the radiators
were going full blast, and it was oppressively hot.*

*"Do you ever fantasize about us being trapped on a desert island
together?" said Hollis.*

"Not really."

"We could catch fish," he said. "Maybe weave some mats."

"I don't eat fish."

"We could pick coconuts. Actually, I can't stand coconuts."

She raised her eyebrows at him over her laptop.

"It was a sweet idea," she said.

More snow fell down past the window.

Hollis didn't have a watch, but he guessed he had another
minute before he had to meet Peters. He closed his eyes and put
his hands over them. A gust of wind rattled the windows, and he
shivered.

*You are in a small rectangular chamber.
A pair of French doors looks East out onto a courtyard.
There are two doorways, leading West and South.*

When he got back to the stairs Peters was waiting, leaning against
the scroll of the banister.

"Anything?"

"Nope," said Hollis. "Sorry."

They were still wearing their coats, and Hollis put his hands
in his pockets. Peters turned and started limping up the stairs.

"Walk this way."

On the second floor a polished wooden railing ran all the
way around the edge of the stairwell, beginning and ending in
little spirals, and overhead there was a grand ceiling with a chan-

delier. Hallways led off into the depths of the house on either side.

"Welcome to the Next Level," said Hollis.

"Shh."

Peters put his fingers to his lips.

"They're somewhere around here," he whispered. "Somewhere near. The bedroom. I forget exactly where."

They chose a direction at random and walked until they found a door. It opened onto a long rectangular library. Peters made a show of peering in around the doorway and motioning Hollis to come in after him. The room was dimly lit by a torchère halogen lamp. Bookshelves ran floor to ceiling, filled mostly with old red-leather-bound Complete Works with gilt lettering on their spines.

Peters opened a drawer in one of the cabinets and rummaged around. He took out a box of condoms.

"Look," he said, holding it up. "We're in the Library of Love."

He put it back and sank down heavily in an armchair. He looked tired.

"Help me, Gamera! Gamera is the friend of all children. Why are we doing this again?"

"Alienation," said Hollis. "Don't you remember? It's the zeitgeist. We're victims of the *fin de siècle*."

"Who's alienated? I'm not alienated."

"I am."

"No, really?" said Peters. "Is that a fact? Hey, what's that thing in your pocket? You aren't still carrying around that beer, are you?"

"What, this?"

Hollis took his hand out of his pocket. He was holding a black leather blackjack with a wooden handle.

"Just a little health insurance," he said.

"Jesus Christ!" said Peters.

He stood up again.

"What the fuck is that thing? Do you want to go up on armed robbery, or something? What's the matter with you?"

It was almost full daylight outside. A strong white light was pushing its way into the room around the edges of the blinds.

"It's technically nonlethal," said Hollis. Peters snorted.

"Well, put it away. What do you think this is, *Fists of Fury*? Where'd you get it, anyway?"

Hollis hefted it experimentally, slapping it against his palm. The leather of the pouch was filled with heavy round pellets that felt like buckshot.

"Some pawnshop. A couple of months ago."

"What for?"

"Beats me. It was an impulse buy. Point-of-purchase."

"Super," said Peters. He lay back in the armchair again and closed his eyes.

Hollis went back to work. He went through a pair of secretary desks, but he found only papers: bank statements, insurance papers, tax forms, birth certificates. When he was done he carefully closed the last drawer and checked the clock on the wall, which was brass and shaped like a barometer. It was 6:07. Birds chirped outside. Next to the clock hung a painting of a clipper ship on a windy day, with its sails flying, caught in the middle of mounting a long, blue-green swell chased with shreds of white foam.

Hollis read the title out loud to himself.

"Flying Cloud. Beating to Windward."

"You said 'beat,'" said Peters.

"Maybe I should run away to sea."

Peters snorted again.

"Don't laugh," said Hollis. "I think they still have merchant marines, somewhere. Or something like that."

Somewhere down the hall, a door opened and closed.

For a long second neither of them moved.

"Uh-oh," Peters whispered. "Did you hear that?"

Hollis nodded.

Before he could say anything, Peters was up and tiptoeing over to the door. He looked both ways, then slipped silently out into the hall.

When Hollis looked out into the corridor it was empty. Peters was already at the far end, peering around the corner.

"What are you doing?" Hollis called after him, in a hoarse whisper.

He was doomed if the Devilfish reached the open sea. It would take him out into the depths and drown him.

Peters glanced back at him for a second without answering, then disappeared around the corner. When Hollis reached the corner he saw that the hall went on much farther, back into one of the rear wings, with a series of identical doors on either side. Peters was making his way forward along the wall step by step, crouched down.

"Where are you going?" Hollis whispered, but too softly for Peters to hear him.

They heard another door closing, from farther down the hall, and Peters froze, then ducked into a doorway on the right. Hollis was left standing by himself in plain sight. The far end of the hall was barely visible in the dimness. He walked farther up, to where Peters was hiding.

He was in a tiny pink-and-blue-tiled bathroom, standing in the bathtub. He put his head out from behind the pink shower curtain.

"Lock it," Hollis whispered, miming turning a doorknob, and Peters nodded. He closed the door, and Hollis stepped back into the hall. The latch clicked.

The hall was still empty. There was a framed poster hanging on the wall next to the bathroom door, a Monet painting of a haystack. Hollis went over to it and turned it around to face the wall. He took a pen out of his pocket and wrote

NE TRAVAILLEZ JAMAIS

in big block letters on the brown paper backing. Then he stepped back into an open doorway.

Somewhere in the house the furnace switched itself off with a loud *click*, followed by silence. His throat tickled, and he had to fight back the urge to cough.

For a minute nothing happened.

I had this dream where we were all on the Enterprise

Just when he was about to check the hall again, he heard a footstep on the carpet a few feet away.

Mr. Donnelly was standing in front of him.

He was very fat. He faced away from Hollis, looking at the door of the bathroom where Peters was hiding. Hollis held his breath. Mr. Donnelly's shoulders were broad and very red, with symmetrical patches of dark hair on them. There was a rip in his underwear, and his sleeveless white undershirt had sweat stains under the arms. His calves were pale and bristly above his black socks.

Hollis kept his hand on the blackjack in the pocket of his overcoat.

I had this dream

Mr. Donnelly put his hand on the doorknob of the little bathroom. Hollis tensed. After a second he seemed to change his mind, and he took it back. He looked over at the picture that was hanging facing the wall and reached out and took it in both hands. Moving with exaggerated carefulness, as if he were still half asleep, he turned it back around again and took a step back to look at it, to make sure it was level. Hollis could hear the noise of his deep, calm breathing.

Then he turned and started shuffling back down the hall the way he came. Hollis stepped out of the doorway and stood behind him.

The sun is going down on a salt marsh. The tide carries a skiff faster and faster out to sea.

These aren't the droids you're looking for.

Mr. Donnelly moved slowly, like a sleepwalker, his heavy bulk swaying a little from side to side as he walked. Standing in the middle of the hall, gripping the blackjack in his pocket, Hollis watched him go. He turned the corner and was out of sight.

Come get some, sugar.

Hollis looked over at the picture again. His heart was racing, and he was having trouble breathing, as if he'd just been running hard. He took in a long, unsteady lungful of air, then let it out again.

A post marks the channel to the ocean.

The bathroom door opened, and Peters looked out. He was breathing hard too.

"What happened?" he whispered.

"Not too fucking much."

"I was behind the shower curtain." He put his hand on his chest. "Held my breath. What do you think?"

"I doubt he's coming back."

Peters nodded, and he looked over at the doorway where Hollis had been standing.

"What's in there?" he whispered.

"I don't know. Looks like somebody's study."

Peters went over and looked inside.

"Are you going to check it?" said Hollis.

"Just for a second."

"I'll keep watch."

Said the Joker to the Thief.

"You do that."

Hollis waited at the door while Peters searched. He threw back the curtains, revealing a full view of the front lawn: the grass was already visibly green in the thin early-morning light, and the miniature lamppost had been turned off. Hollis could hear him going through the room at top speed, opening and shutting drawers and swearing, pushing aside clothes hangers in the closet, wrestling a drawer out of its slot. He leaned his head back until it rested against the wall. His eyes closed.

Something in his mind clicked, and he opened them again. He went back over to the Monet poster and pushed his hand up behind it: there, in one corner, he could feel two keys taped to the brown paper backing. He ripped them off. The keys were bronze-colored, and someone had written HOUSE along the tape in blue ballpoint pen.

"Dude," he said urgently. "Come here."

He snapped his fingers, and Peters stopped searching and came out of the study.

"What is it?"

Hollis tossed him the keys, and Peters caught them one-handed.

"When a thief thieves a thief," said Hollis, "God laughs."

Peters just stood there for a second, turning them over in his hand.

"Jesus," he said, unbelievingly. He looked up at Hollis. "Let's get the hell out of here."

He shoved the keys in his pocket and started walking quickly down the hall back towards the stairs. Hollis checked the hall in the other direction, but it was clear. When he turned back, Peters had started to run.

Hollis jogged after him. The first floor had been dark when they first searched it, but now the curtains glowed with the sunlight behind them. Hollis walked through the entrance hall into the dining room, where he found his can of beer where he had left it on the table. He took it with him. In the kitchen the clock in the microwave said 6:18. He scooped up the rest of the six-pack from off the counter. They were frosted with moisture, and he swiped away the wet rings with his sleeve.

Peters was already waiting for him in the little storage room. Hollis carefully closed the heavy inner door behind him.

"Quick, Marty!" he said hoarsely. "Back to the DeLorean!"

Outside on the landing they had to blink their eyes against the light. There was no frost, but it was chilly, and water glittered coldly on the grass. Hollis took a moment to wrap his coat more tightly around him before he stepped off the porch. They jogged across the lawn and part of the way down the street before they gave it up and slowed down to a walk.

"Jesus," Peters said. "I think I'm going to have an embolism."

Hollis felt dizzy. It had been a couple of days since he'd had a real meal. He touched his chin with his hand: he was already growing a thin, straggly goatee. It was an effort to keep walking straight; he glanced over at Peters, but he didn't seem to notice. Yellow and red leaves settled and spun their way down through the clear air.

A Volvo station wagon was warming up in the driveway of the Victorian farmhouse across the street, sending up a plume of white exhaust, but the driver paid no attention to them. When they got to the Lexus, Peters unlocked it, and Hollis squeezed in past the fir tree on the passenger side. The moment he sat down he felt completely drained, and he let his head loll back against the headrest.

"You okay with driving?" he said.

"Of course."

"I feel like fucking hell," Hollis said. "God, look at all this fucking daylight — it's so disgustingly cheery."

Peters started the engine, and the headlights came on, pale and weak in the early-morning light. He snapped them off.

"Guess we won't be needing those." He cleared his throat. "You want a cigarette?"

"God, no. Is there any food in this thing?"

Peters shrugged, released the brake, and cranked the wheel all the way to the left. He pulled out into a tight U-turn. The street was wide and empty, and he floored it.

"Slow down!" he said, to himself. "You'll get us all killed!"

Hollis sniffed.

"So are you going to call that girl?" said Peters. "The one you met at Amanda's?"

"Jesus, I already told you, I went out with her. It didn't fly."

"You could still call her," said Peters.

Hollis looked out the window at the houses.

"I would prefer not to discuss the matter further."

With his eyes half open, Hollis watched the scenery fly by. For a long time neither of them said anything. There was forest on either side, pine trees, and signs for frost heaves and deer crossings. He couldn't tell if they were taking the same route as before or a new one.

He closed his eyes.

When they got to the center of town they came up on a yellow school bus, and Peters stopped to wait for it. He nudged Hollis. A high school girl was hurrying to catch it, coming towards them along the sidewalk.

"Look at that."

She had a pale, clear oval face and ringlety brown hair that fell down to her shoulders. She wore her backpack with the straps over both shoulders, and she jogged towards the bus with her thumbs hooked behind the straps. Hollis watched her getting on.

"*La beauté*," he said, "*c'est la promesse de bonheur*."

"She's more your type, chum," said Peters. "One of those Andie McDowell types."

Shall I have her sent round to the castle, milord?
Aye. And see that she's given a good bath first.

When they reached the on-ramp to the highway, Peters took it without slowing down.

"Hand me my shades, would you?" he said. "I think they're in the glove compartment."

Hollis found them. Peters put them on in front of his little round glasses and looked at himself in the rearview mirror.

"I am become a Callow Youth," he said solemnly.

They were in the commuter rush from the suburbs into Boston, but it was too early for the highway to be very crowded.

Accelerating up to highway speed, Peters reclined the seat a notch and leaned back.

"I can't believe people are going to work now," said Hollis.

"Mm." Peters shook his fist at the other cars. "Do you people know you're *alive*? Crawling along, in your little metal coffins—"

Hollis reached down to where the beer was, around his feet, and opened a can. He toasted them discreetly.

When they reached the entrance ramp to the turnpike the traffic became heavier, and Peters slowed down. For a long time the highway ran between two huge cliffs of bare red rock, with slicks of water running down them where blasting had exposed underground springs.

Hollis's eyes blurred, and he didn't even notice they were back in the city until they drove under the bridge into Allston. Harvard Avenue was congested, and they inched along it towards the intersection with Brighton.

"Where are you going to park?" said Hollis.

"I don't know." Peters rubbed his eyes with his free hand. "Probably I'll just put it in the lot across from Blake's and walk home."

"I have that 'Video Killed the Radio Star' song in my head. I can't get it out."

"Whoa," said Peters. "Eighties kitsch alert."

There was a slow light at the corner of Commonwealth. Hollis watched the people crossing in front of them on the crosswalk.

With the light behind it her blond hair was dark.

Peters drove a few extra blocks up the hill and made a U-turn to get on the right side of the street in front of Hollis's stoop. When they finally pulled up, Peters backed into a space, jostling the car behind him with his bumper.

Looking up, they both noticed at the same time that the sky was full of birds, smallish and black, swarms of them, crossing above the street in great, silent waves that constantly changed their size and shape. Each individual stood out clearly and distinctly against the white background of the sky. Hollis and Peters watched for a minute or so, looking up blearily through the windshield, until the flock had dwindled down to a thin scattering, then a couple of isolated groups, and then finally a few frantic stragglers flapping desperately along after the others.

"Geese," said Peters.

"Can't be," said Hollis. "Geese are way bigger than that. And don't they fly in V's?"

"I guess. I wasn't really sure if that was a myth or not."

Hollis opened the door.

"Anyway, I'll see you tonight."

"I'll call you," said Peters.

"Right."

He shut the door behind him, and Peters gave him a *bra* sign through the window.

It was disorienting to be out in the cold on the sidewalk in the early morning — the sunlight seemed to be coming at him from the wrong side. Peters peeled out, dead leaves flying up into the air in his wake. An old woman who lived in the building was on her way out as Hollis went in, and she nodded and murmured something to him in a Russian accent.

I am an android, a sophisticated computer endowed with the form of a human simulacrum.

When Hollis reached his door, he realized he didn't have his keys. He checked his pants pockets, and his overcoat, but they weren't there. He tried to remember what he'd done with them — he'd taken them out of his pocket and put them somewhere, but now he couldn't seem to remember where. He stood there for a few minutes in the darkness of the hallway, with his hand on his forehead. He was very tired. The tiny glass-and-metal eye of the peephole stared dully back at him. He looked down at the scratched wood around the keyhole on his door, then up and down the empty, badly lit hallway.

After a long time, he put his hand on the doorknob and pushed in on it, without turning.

The door opened.

CHAPTER 8

FRIDAY, 3:30 P.M.

It was three-thirty in the afternoon, and Hollis was standing waiting for the Green Line trolley. It was overcast. Cars tore past him in both directions. It was Friday — people were getting out of work early to start the weekend.

He stood inside a plastic shelter on the platform. There was a subway map on the wall, covered with un-readable black graffiti signatures written with a paint pen. Hollis took a scrap of paper out of his pocket and checked it against the map. It was a page torn out of a road atlas. He'd circled one of the intersections on it with a Magic Marker.

He still needed a shave, but he felt better now that he'd slept. He'd gotten up at three, taken a shower, and had some breakfast. The sun was already low on the horizon behind the clouds. Looking back up the hill, he could see the single oversized headlight of the inbound train shining in the distance, still half a mile away, but it would take five more minutes for it to work its way down to where he was waiting.

A circle of old retirees was standing around under the shelter next to him.

"Yeah, I gave it to her," said a white-haired, red-faced man. "I said, 'Listen, you wanna talk about rubbers? Save it for the bridge club.' "

They broke up laughing.

"You told her."

"I certainly did. 'Save it for the bridge club,' I said."

He shook his head.

"She didn't know what to say."

Honest, Officer, he threw himself right onto the tracks. I couldn't stop him.

When the train pulled in it was already mostly filled with sporty, well-fed BC students heading into the city. Hollis got on and rode standing up, hanging on to a steel post, so he could look out the window. The train was incredibly slow — it stopped at every corner, all the way along Commonwealth Ave. into the city.

While it waited at a red light, Hollis spotted a woman about his age standing on the curb with her back to him. Her hair was dyed blond, and it was piled up on top of her head in a careless, complicated, but somehow elegant heap. She was wearing a denim jacket with a giant mandala scribbled on the back in black ballpoint pen.

I read an electron emission signature, sir. A life form.

Let me tek you away from all zees.

The train picked up some speed as they rolled out of the residential neighborhood into BU, and the clacking of the wheels accelerated and crescendoed. From where he was standing Hollis could look down into the interiors of the cars moving along past him, and down onto the sidewalks, where assorted college students were pushing past each other, wearing sweaters and carrying their books and backpacks: punks, jocks, artsy types, frat boys.

Soon your pitiful little planet will be mine. Oh yes—quite soon.

The tracks sloped down, cement walls rose up in the windows on both sides, and suddenly the train was underground. Hollis's reflection appeared in front of him in the window against the blackness of the tunnel. Every couple of minutes the lights would flicker out for a second or two, leaving the car in a dimness that was strangely intimate: it was a small, dark room full of strangers.

More and more of the people getting on and off were wearing office clothes. Hollis got out at Government Center, five stops down the line. His car ended up at the back end of the platform, and he had to walk a ways to get to an exit. The station walls were covered with sweating white porcelain tiles. A long escalator took him up to the empty lobby, where the ceiling was made of translucent plastic panels, each one a slightly different shade of white. A giant Calder-style mobile hung motionless from the ceiling.

When he stepped out of the subway station he found himself on the corner of a huge, open brick plaza. It was deserted except for a few vendors selling flowers and newspapers and hot pretzels. Litter slid and tumbled across it in the freezing wind. Flags from different countries flapped on a row of white flagpoles.

Hollis set off across the square. The air felt colder and brisker here, and it tasted salty — he was getting close to the sea. Clouds of fine, powdery dust swirled across the bare brick. One of the cafés on the square had a giant metal teakettle mounted on its storefront. Real steam was coming out of the spout.

Hollis took out the piece of paper again and looked at it as he walked. He turned it around a few times, until it was oriented the same way he was, then he put it away.

I have seen the best minds of my generation

He cut through Quincy Market, threading his way through crowds of tourists without slowing down. A tall, skinny magician in a tuxedo was doing tricks with ropes and knots in the middle of a ring of spectators. The peripheral highway that ran along the docks came up suddenly, only a block past the market. There was nowhere to cross it legally, but he waited on the shoulder for a while for a break in traffic, surrounded by broken glass and black, charred-looking blowout pads.

"You can't ride back in the rain, Hollis. Wait a few minutes."

"I can't exactly stay here, can I?" he said bitterly. "Anyway, it's not raining anymore."

"Yes, it is."

"No, it isn't."

Eileen went over to the window and pulled up the blinds. They looked out through the black bars of the fire escape. Night was falling.

"Is it?" said Hollis. "I can't really tell."

"I guess I can't tell either."

They listened for the sound of rain.

"Anyway," she said. "Take an umbrella."

The road cleared for a minute. He jogged across a few lanes of black asphalt worn shiny with age, jumped over a guardrail, and suddenly he was at the docks. Two enormous splintery gray timber wharfs jutted out into the harbor in front of him. The New England Aquarium stood at the end of them, on a double row of massive concrete pilings.

A scum of foam and floating trash bobbed around the base of the pilings, but farther out in the main harbor the water was blue and clean. The air was chilly. Seagulls wheeled and cried overhead. Hollis could see as far as Logan Airport on the far side of the bay, where every couple of minutes another plane took off or landed, weirdly out of sync with the roar of its engine because of the time delay as the sound traveled across the harbor. Tiny indigo-blue lights winked on and off, all along the runways.

You weel tek me to Cuba.

It took him a few minutes to walk out to the end of the wharfs; they were longer than they looked. It was late afternoon, and there was no line at the ticket booth. The woman at the register had straight red hair, and her oval face was startlingly pale and colorless, like an ivory cameo. She looked up from the paperback she was reading: *Culture and Anarchy.*

"Just one today?" she said.

Hollis nodded.

"You know, we'll be closing in about an hour."

"That's all right," he said. He took out his wallet and opened it. It was empty.

He took out his Visa.

"Can I charge this?" he said. She took his card, zipped it through a reader, and handed it back with the credit card form and a ballpoint pen.

My good woman, have you any idea what this signature might one day be worth?

He pushed his way inside through the heavy glass doors. The aquarium was set up in one long spiral ramp that sloped gently upwards, with the tanks arranged along the walls on both sides in no particular order. The rest of the visitors were mostly children with their parents or in groups from their schools. The constant shouting made an echoey roar in the darkness. They paid no attention to Hollis as he drifted through them.

The only light came from the tanks themselves, but as his eyes adapted Hollis was able to make out the faces of the people around him in the soft, TV-like glow that filtered out through the water. He strolled past the first few tanks, looking over the shoulders of the people clustered around them. The fish that lived close to the surface had tanks built to look like sunny ponds or tide pools, with bright lights overhead and sand and fake reeds around the edges, but most of the tanks were darker, more somber, to simulate conditions farther underwater. The weird, distorted fish that lived in the deepest strata of the ocean were kept in almost total darkness. Sometimes Hollis had to stare at a tank for a few minutes before the outlines of a giant grouper finally appeared in the gloom, or a horrible flounder, or a few floating nautiluses.

Halfway up, the spiral ramp opened out into a landing with some displays on it for children, and a counter with a row of flimsy cardboard zoetrope wheels. Hollis went over to one and put his eye up to the viewing slot. He spun it.

Inside, a tiny black-and-white line drawing of a ray frantically flapped its wings up and down in jerky stop-motion animation.

The Devilfish!

Hollis stood up sharply. He looked around, blinking. The roar of the crowd went on around him without stopping, and a kid behind him was waiting to look. He stepped aside.

Watch for the sign of the black fish.

Wandering slowly up the spiraling ramp, Hollis stopped at every tank, one by one. The air had a nice, humid, briny smell. Most of the interesting exhibits were from the tropics: a pack of piranhas floating together peacefully in a South American stream; a forest of fluorescent anemones, with huge spidery prawns wandering through it; an octopus huddled in the corner of a bare glass cell.

"Choose carefully," said the old man. "Each gateway leads to a different world."

Hollis spent a long time watching a tank that was split into two parts, half air and half water. It was supposed to be a tropical rainforest that had been flooded by a seasonal monsoon. Big, fleshy fishes floated around in it like toy balloons, drifting between the giant buttress roots of plastic trees, wavering their tiny fins almost imperceptibly to keep themselves upright. Fake vines lolled along the surface of the water, and tree frogs clung to the leaves of fake jungle plants. He moved on.

When he reached the top floor the hallway started sloping back down again, and one whole wall was taken up by the aquarium's main attraction: an enormous round tank that ran the full height of the building. The fish swam around and around the outer edge of the tank in endless, hypnotic circles, all in the same direction, accompanied by sea turtles and a few long, sinewy sharks. As Hollis walked slowly around and down, the light from the tank gradually grew deeper and softer, greener, dreamier. A massive emerald moray eel drifted by, undulating itself sideways through the coral crags. He found himself becoming more and more thoroughly entranced.

Near the bottom of the tank — he could see the sandy floor a few meters farther down — some kind of commotion started back up at the surface. Something was splashing around, children were shrieking happily, and an amplified voice was giving some kind of educational lecture. The angle was bad, but way up above him, through the green haze, he thought he could see a pair of bare pink legs dangling down through the shifting, mirrorlike undersurface of the water.

Then the person plunged the rest of the way through: it was a scuba diver. She sank down for a few seconds, passively, getting her bearings and waiting for the bubbles to clear, and then she started swimming, carefully merging herself into the flow of the circulating throng of fish. She had a mesh bag slung around her neck, and she started feeding the sharks from it, passing out chunks of bait with a kind of sowing motion. The sharks would nose up to her and take them right from her hand, flashing multiple rows of gray teeth at her for one thrilling moment and then moving on again with an indifferent, businesslike air.

Hollis watched for a minute, then started walking again. He lost track of the diver's progress. Then a pair of black rubber flippers appeared at the top of the window, followed by a pair of long, slender, bare legs, and a torso in a form-fitting black wet suit.

Her face was level with his, and their eyes met through the glass. Hollis froze.

It was Xanthe.

The mask covered most of her face, not particularly attractively, but there was no question who it was. She didn't react — in fact, she seemed to look right through him. She blinked once, but she made no sign that she recognized him. As he stared back at her Hollis wondered if Xanthe could even see him through the thick glass of the tank. She went past him in slow motion, dropping gracefully down through the water, looking out at him without seeming to register his presence at all, and when she was almost gone he reached out across the railing and tapped gently on the glass, once, twice, with his fingertips, but it was too late. The last streamers of her hair were trailing out of sight. He pressed his forehead up against the warm glass, but all he could see was the top of her head, retreating down and away from him.

The truth hurts.

A woman's voice was speaking over the loudspeakers: the aquarium would be closing in ten minutes. Hollis walked the rest of the way down to the lobby without stopping, or even glancing at the tank.

When he pushed back out through the front doors it was nearly five o'clock, and the cloudy sunlight was getting weaker. He could see it was only a few more minutes before the sun would disappear behind the downtown skyscrapers. Hollis stood in front of the glass doors, arms folded, squinting at the sudden brightness and watching the families sitting around on benches around a green pool where a few tame harbor seals were playing.

It was cold out. He hugged his green overcoat around him.

It was late by the time he knocked on Eileen's door.

"Hollis," she said, when she opened it. "Listen—"

"Wait." He held up his hands. "Please wait. Just wait a second."

She closed the door behind him and went over and sat down on the bed. Her weight caused one of the pillows to topple over the edge onto the floor.

"I'm waiting," she said.

"Just give me a second—"

"Hollis—"

"Would you just give me a second, please?" he said, exasperatedly. "Could I please finish what I was going to say, before you break up with me?"

He went over to the bed and sat down next to her. Her room had a certain characteristic smell, because of a special shampoo she used.

He didn't say anything.

After a little while she took his hand, without looking at him.

"Hollis? Can we be serious for a minute?"

The wind blew straight through Hollis's short blond hair, chilling his scalp. He went over to the railing looking out over the harbor and kicked some sand off the pavement to watch it splash into the water. Helium-voiced children talked and yelled as they filed out of the aquarium. Long, gentle swells rolled in through the harbor mouth, coming in from the open ocean and sweeping on past the wooden pilings without slowing down, moving out of sight underneath him to break against the cement of the harbor wall.

The time for waiting is past.

We must act now.

CHAPTER 9

Hollis walked quickly along the sidewalk away from the docks with a cigarette in his mouth. He broke into a jog for a few seconds, then lapsed back into a walk again. He struck a match, but it went out before he could get the cigarette lit. He tore off another one. The sidewalk ran underneath an elevated highway held up by giant steel pylons painted an oxidized green. They made a line of nested square green archways that receded into the distance, seemingly to infinity.

The match went out again, and he lit another one. It was almost dusk, and Hollis turned down a narrow street, deep in the shadow of the office buildings on either side of it. A single-file line of traffic was backed up along it, and some of the cars had their lights on. They barely fit between the double row of parked cars along both curbs. It was a wealthy neighborhood, and the sidewalk was neat and swept. Hollis stopped and took the crumpled piece of paper out of his pocket again to check the address.

Pulling his overcoat tighter, he turned his back to the wind and lit another match. This time it stayed lit long enough for him to get the cigarette going, and he took a deep drag and checked his reflection in a car window.

He was so transformed that she no longer recognized the dashing young man who had once been her lover.

Outside a bank a clock with a glowing face was mounted on a fluted classical column: it was almost five.

"Fucking hell," he said.

He stopped at a bank of pay phones on the corner and dug in his pockets until he came up with a crumpled business card and twenty-five cents in loose change. The traffic was noisy, and he had to punch the volume button a couple of times before he could hear the dial tone.

Hollis could feel his fingers getting cold as he dialed. It rang five times before somebody picked up.

"Houghton Mifflin, how can I help you?"

It was a woman's voice.

"Hi," said Hollis. "Is Bob Rice there, please?"

"I'm sorry, Bob's gone home for the weekend. Can I have him give you a call back?"

Hollis pinched the bridge of his nose between his fingers.

"Ah — I guess it doesn't matter. Is he coming in tomorrow?"

"I don't think so," she said. "He doesn't usually work weekends."

"Right. Okay."

There was a pause. Hollis stubbed out his cigarette on the side of the pay phone.

"Well, thanks," he said. "I guess I'll try him again on Monday."

Domo arigato.

"All right," said the woman. "Bye now."

"Bye."

Hollis hung up. He took a deep breath and leaned back against the side of the payphone.

He watched the traffic. It was still backed up, and he could smell the pleasantly intense smell of the exhaust from the idling motors. A lot of the cars were expensive — BMWs, Porsches, Saabs, a limousine, all painted expensive-looking blacks and creams and dark greens. Down the street a ways a man stood with his black leather shoe propped up unsteadily on a chain, tying it and whistling.

Hollis stood up and started walking again.

The street went uphill. Heading away from the harbor, farther into the city, he could already see the green grass of Boston Common in the far distance, where State Street ended. The dome of the Old State House rose up in the distance, covered in golden panels. Most of the buildings had kept their antique fittings: door knockers, ornate lampposts, wrought-iron boot scrapers. The trees planted along the sidewalk were bolted down with wire stays. As he walked Hollis searched for his reflection in the wall of a polished black granite bank.

My God—it's full of stars.

He lit another cigarette. The stores were mostly trendy business-lunch eateries and boutiquey chain stores — French

Connection, Ann Taylor, Armani A/X. A male-model type with a long blond ponytail and a leather jacket waited by the curb, sitting on a fat chugging motorcycle with a huge rack of red lights on the back. Hollis started to walk faster, stiff-legged. He took another drag on the cigarette and coughed.

He got there sooner than he expected. The building was a modern-looking skyscraper, fifty or sixty stories tall; Hollis had to step back to the edge of the sidewalk to see the very top. The address was spelled out over the doors in shiny brass sans serif letters:

SEVENTY-FIVE STATE STREET

An airy smoked-glass lobby took up the first few floors. A few scattered lights were on in the upper stories. A seagull wheeled and circled around the very top. Behind it featureless white clouds rolled by in the darkening blue sky.

Sometimes, towards evening, a lone figure would appear on the ancient battlements, gazing out at the horizon.

The next building over housed an HMV, and Hollis strolled over and looked in the front window. There was an elaborate cardboard display promoting a Liz Phair album, and a music video was showing on a TV monitor, with no sound.

He went inside, and the same song was playing over the loudspeakers. He watched the rest of the video on a stack of TVs set up on one wall, all networked together to make one big picture, then walked upstairs where the CDs were. He walked around the aisles at random and looked through the magazines. There was a Sega game system set up on a display stand, hooked up to a big-screen TV, and he turned it on.

A menu of games popped up:

```
PLUNDER: THE VENGEANCE
CODEX
AGE OF IRON
PGA GOLF SUPER-PRO
ECCO THE DOLPHIN
TASKMASTER
```

Hollis clicked on ECCO THE DOLPHIN.

It took him a minute to figure out the controls — there didn't seem to be any directions anywhere — but the game was mostly self-explanatory. He was a dolphin, swimming around underwater, on a quest to rescue his fellow sea creatures, who'd been kidnapped by mysterious and powerful forces. He swam around collecting clues and exploring secret chambers, where he could consult older and wiser sea creatures who offered him cryptic advice. He started to concentrate. There were obstacles to contend with: sharks, jellyfish, a time limit on how long he could stay underwater without breathing. If he got up enough speed he could leap out of the water into the air, with an animated blue sky behind him. Hypnotic, new-agey mood music played in the background. Every time he found something new the game allowed him farther into the labyrinth, and without realizing it he started bending over the controls, totally absorbed.

The screen went dark.

It took him a few seconds to figure out what was going on. The game had turned itself off — there was some kind of built-in limit on how long one could play. He blinked and looked around: a couple of teenagers were standing behind him waiting to use it. As he put the joystick back on the cardboard rack his hands were shaking. He shoved them in his pockets and headed back downstairs. Outside, in the window, he saw that night was falling.

Our world is dying. Only you can save us.

Hollis walked back over to 75 State Street. A few older men and women were on their way out, buttoning their coats and tossing their scarves over their shoulders as the cold hit them. They didn't acknowledge him as he went by. For some reason the burnished-metal revolving door was incredibly heavy, and Hollis found himself having to plant his feet and lean into it to get it moving.

Inside it was warm and humid and weirdly quiet, like a greenhouse: the glass walls instantly cut off all noise from the street. He looked up: the ceiling was three or four stories above him. Groves of delicate birch saplings stood in the corners in ceramic tubs, with obsidian slab benches neatly arranged underneath them. Hollis could hear the whisper of some kind of high-tech ventilation system hushing subsonically in the background.

I'm tired.

He walked through towards the back, in the direction of a bank of elevators. A security guard in a blue rent-a-cop uniform stopped him. She was sitting behind a semicircular marble desk.

"Sign in, please," she said. "It's after five."

She pushed a battered black binder towards him across the desktop, with a ballpoint pen on a chain.

"Sure," said Hollis. His voice sounded far away. He signed.

Have you any idea how much this signature

A list of the tenant companies was posted on the wall behind the guard, and he checked it and walked past her. Munson, Hanson, Gund was on the twenty-first floor. An elevator was already waiting, and in the second before the polished-brass doors opened he caught a glimpse of his reflection in them, distorted by the wavy metal and divided down the middle by the center line.

The elevator was empty. The lighting inside was bright and harsh: a modern-looking grid of spotlights mounted on the ceiling. He closed his eyes. With his fingertips, he felt the metal nubs of the floor numbers written in Braille under the buttons.

Eileen always knew there was something special about that Kessler boy, and when

It only took a few seconds. The bell rang, and the doors opened directly onto the office anteroom: apparently the company owned the whole floor. The anteroom was decorated like an old-fashioned cloakroom, with wood paneling and an umbrella stand. He walked through it into a reception area, which was painted a stylish but soothing rose color. The receptionist, a young woman with brown hair, looked up when he came in.

I am an android, Doctor. I am incapable of experiencing fear.

She was sitting on an uncomfortable-looking orthopedic chair with no back, wearing a headset phone.

"Can I help you?" she said.

Why, Mr. Kessler is one of our most valuable clients.

Hollis cleared his throat.

"I'm looking for Eileen Cavanaugh."

"I'll see if she's free," said the woman.

She switched to an intercom and politely lowered her voice. "Darcy? Is Eileen there? There's someone out here to see her." She listened for an answer, then looked back up at Hollis. "Your name?" she said.

Call me Ishmael.

He cleared his throat.
"Scotty."
She waited for a moment for Hollis to give a last name, but when he didn't she just said "Scotty" into the headset, then stopped and listened again, tapping her pen.
"Thanks, Darcy." The receptionist looked up. "She's with somebody right now, Scotty, but she should be free in another minute. If you'd like to take a seat, you can wait right over there."
She indicated an overstuffed brown leather couch, and he walked over and sat down. He crossed his legs until one of his feet started to get numb, then he crossed them the other way. The receptionist went on with her conversation. Hollis stared straight ahead at the opposite wall. The coffee table was covered with business and investment magazines.

The fishing was very bad. Tonga's family had nothing to eat.

"Do you have an appointment?"
"What?"
He looked up.
"Do you have an appointment?" said the secretary. "With Eileen?"
The monitor on the desk next to her was angled to one side, displaying an incredibly complicated-looking spreadsheet document.

"It's supposed to be a surprise."

"Well, she should be done in just a couple of minutes."

She looked down again. If Hollis craned his neck he could see a hall that led farther back into the company suite.

Another minute went by. Finally, in response to some signal that only she could perceive, the receptionist looked up again, flashed him a tiny fake smile, and motioned to him to go in through the door.

Once he was inside, he wasn't sure exactly where he was supposed to be going. None of the doors seemed to be labeled, and he couldn't seem to force himself to ask any of the people he passed. He kept walking blindly straight ahead until he reached the end of the hallway. It opened out into another waiting room, which was an almost perfect replica of the first one.

The first thing he heard as he came into the room was Eileen's voice.

The receptionist didn't say anything. She just pointed to a couch, and Hollis sat down again, but his skin was prickling. He felt preternaturally alert. He couldn't see her, and he couldn't quite make out what she was saying, but he was sure he recognized her tone of voice, which was very distinctive: Eileen had a very cool, very reasonable way of speaking, which would accelerate every once in a while up to a momentary pitch of overexcitement, getting higher and faster at the same time, then decline again just as quickly into an even, regular calmness. Hollis shifted over on the couch a little for a better angle on where the sound was coming from. There she was, standing with her back to him in a doorway at the far end of the hall. He couldn't make out who she was talking to. Light from inside the room was spilling out around her, making a silhouette. He watched her for a long time without moving.

She stood with her arms folded, wearing a dark green cashmere sweater over a short, stylish black dress and black stockings. Her blond hair was short and wavy. He'd forgotten how small she was.

Then she turned around and started walking down the hall towards him, still talking back over her shoulder:

"Back in a minute," she called musically.

She was walking briskly, in a hurry. He could see her face now: her features were very fine, a little aristocratic, quirkily pretty. She had an open face, with a tiny pointed nose and just the hint of a double chin.

When she saw him, she stopped.

"Well," she said.

She put her hands on her hips.

"Well, well, well." Eileen walked slowly out into the room. "If it isn't Scotty Kessler."

Hollis was still sitting down, and she leaned down and kissed him lightly on the cheek.

"How's tricks down in Engineering, Scotty?"

He looked up at her from the couch. She was freshly made up, and she smelled like perfume. He didn't think he could stand up.

With the light behind it her blond hair was dark.

"Not bad," he said hoarsely.

He cleared his throat.

"I can't work miracles."

"I haven't seen you for ages," she said, and she canted her head to one side. "You've been underground. Everybody's looking for you, you know — people talk about you like you're some kind of leprechaun. You're not even in Information."

"I know."

She sat down sideways on the couch next to him, a comfortable distance away, and slipping off her shoe, she tucked one stockinged leg up under her, girlishly.

"So you still live in Boston?"

He nodded.

"I was just walking around. I remembered your address."

"I'm so glad," she said. "It's good to see you."

"I like your office."

She chuckled and glanced up at the ceiling.

"Don't try to snow me, Mr. Big-Time Anarchist. I know there are visions of Molotov cocktails dancing in your head even as we speak."

"No, really," he said. "It looks like a nice place to work in. I was expecting something much more — I don't know. Corporate. Productivity-enhancing."

"Well, it isn't really all that bad. You read too much science fiction — it's not *Brazil*, or anything. I'd much rather be in New York, but they gave me a good offer here."

They looked at each other for a few seconds. The receptionist was quietly taking a call.

"So are you working or anything?"

"Not really," said Hollis, and he looked down at the carpet. "I'm looking into a couple of research projects. Freelance stuff."

"Why don't you think about coming here?" said Eileen. Her eyes were a very pale blue. "We're doing all kinds of hiring right now — they're crazy about humanities types. You should send over your résumé."

He smiled wryly.

"Sure."

"I'm *serious*, Hollis — just send it straight to me. Say the word and I'll even have them send a messenger. A big strong man like you needs a job. Straighten up." She punched his biceps with her tiny fist. "Fly right."

"Ouch," said Hollis, rubbing his arm with his other hand. "That's my pitching arm."

"I mean, *I* can't offer you a job, or anything like that, but I could definitely put in a good word for you."

He nodded.

"I guess it's probably a lot of work."

Straighten up. Fly right.

"Sure, you have to put in fifty, sixty hours, at least — everybody does." She shrugged. "I mean, it's not like being in school."

Hollis glanced down at the backs of his hands.

Never meant for toil, that's sure.

"Well, hard work's no substitute for talent, I always say."

"Hollis, you're — " She started to laugh, then broke off, wrinkling her pointy nose. "My God, Hollis, you absolutely reek of cigarette smoke." She leaned forward and snuffed the lapel of his overcoat. "You *never* smoke."

He shrugged.

"It's never too late to start."

"Hm." She raised her eyebrows. "Well, what about that resumé? Do you have one made up?"

"Sure," said Hollis, a little vaguely. "Look, Eileen, what's it like working at a place like this? I mean — Jesus, somehow I just can't picture what it would be *like*."

"Well— " She hesitated. "Look, you don't really want a lecture, do you?"

"It's just — " Hollis met her gaze directly. "It's just that you know I could never have a job like this."

He noticed she was wearing an apple-green ring made out of

some kind of swirly plastic, one that she hadn't owned when they were going out. She turned it around her finger. By now their faces were very close together, and if he leaned forward only very slightly, he could have kissed her.

"No." She put her hand on his arm. "I don't know that, Hollis. The truth is, you *are* going to end up here — it's just going to take you a little longer than it took the rest of us."

She closed her eyes and then opened them again, a slow blink.

"You'll find out," she said. "Sometimes I think you have an overly vivid imagination, Hollis. With some things it's just not worth thinking about them too carefully before they happen. They almost never turn out to be as horrible as you think they will."

She watched him for a few seconds, and he could see her biting the inside of her cheek, but neither of them spoke. The receptionist was pointedly ignoring them.

"I have somebody waiting in my office, Hollis," she said finally. "I have to get back. Why don't you call me on Monday? Do you — ? Wait. Here's my card."

Eileen patted her thighs with both hands, as if she was looking for pockets. She turned to the secretary.

"Darcy, could you — ?"

The secretary nodded instantly and opened her desk drawer.

"We'll make a time. I'll buy you lunch — you're starting to get a little skinny, even for you."

Hollis nodded again, silently.

He was a mysterious figure—arrogant, aristocratic, coldly beautiful, impossible to understand.

Eileen got up, smoothing down her skirt, and took a step back down the hall towards her office. Hollis looked past her: somebody was leaning against the doorframe, waiting for her. He was tall, and he had shoulder-length blond hair.

Hollis realized he recognized him. It was Brian.

Danger, Will Robinson! Danger!

"Not too early," said Hollis expressionlessly, staring past her at him. "I hunt for insects at night."

"We'll work something out. Tuesday, maybe."

She took a step towards the door. For some reason he noticed some bits of dark green fluff that had migrated from her sweater onto the black fabric of her dress.

His vision was unusually acute.

"Do you want to see my office, real quick?" she said brightly, turning around again. "It's right here."

Brian watched him from behind Eileen, over her shoulder, without hostility but also without any kind of warmth, or even recognition. Their eyes met for a second, and Hollis stared back at him for a long moment before Brian finally looked away.

Hollis slowly rubbed the side of his nose with one finger.

"It can wait," he said.

"Call me Monday then?"

"Sure."

She walked away back down the hall, and the office door closed softly behind them.

Hollis stood up.

I met the man himself today. On the moors.

Darcy was still holding out Eileen's card, waiting for him to notice, and he went over and took it from her. Classical music was playing softly over hidden speakers, an overexposed Vivaldi violin concerto, and suddenly, underneath it, Hollis noticed the rustling noise of people working in the offices all around him. It was coming from all sides, directionlessly. The walls were just thin office partitions, and the sound carried right through them: phones ringing, keyboards clattering, people talking. The air reeked of coffee.

Hollis stood still and listened. Betsy watched him disapprovingly. He looked back at her, and then around at the rest of the room, and down the hall at the rows of office doors. One of them opened, and two youngish men in suits came out, talking business animatedly, both holding their camel overcoats draped over the same arm. They were barely older than Hollis. He turned to watch as they swept through the room, nodding to the receptionist, and out the other door in the direction of the elevators.

Hollis's face was blank. He reached up and felt the stubble on his chin, gingerly.

Everybody has something to do.

FRIDAY, 5:45 P.M.

Hollis's boots made an echoey sound on the marble floor of the lobby. As he pushed his way out through the revolving door the security guard yelled after him to sign out, but he didn't turn around. When he was a few blocks away, he took the piece of paper with Eileen's address on it out of his pocket and threw it into a steel trash can, which was twisted and half melted from having had a fire in it.

The air was full of exhaust from the rush-hour traffic. The temperature was dropping, and white fluorescent lights blinked on and off in random sprinkling patterns in the skyscrapers. The closest subway stop was Boylston, at the corner of Boston Common, and Hollis walked there at an even pace, neither hurrying nor lingering. Huge white clouds of steam billowed up out of storm drains and through the finger holes in manhole covers, even through cracks in the street.

Inside the subway station it was cold and crowded, the commuters staring straight ahead, emptily, like refugees in newsreel footage of a war-torn foreign country. Hollis looked down at the tracks from the platform: there was an inch of standing water under the wooden ties. He still wasn't far from the harbor.

When the train came it was almost full, and he had to squeeze himself in. The car rocked gently back and forth on the track. Hollis watched the gray stucco wall of the tunnel fly by, a yard in front of his face. All around him people were talking and shouting over the roar. When the tracks rose above ground at Kenmore Square, after twenty minutes, it got a little quieter.

The neon lights of the clubs went through their regular cycles in the darkness.

By the year 2097 the cities of the Eastern Seaboard had merged to form a single megalopolis of shocking size and squalor.

As the sun went down, the clouds started to glow with the weird orange light of the city. Hollis accidentally met his own eyes in the window and looked away. It was a Friday night, and the subway was free outbound after Kenmore, so wherever the train stopped lines of people on the platforms waited to get on. Each time it took a few minutes to get them all packed in. They stopped and started at every intersection all the way down the length of Commonwealth.

Hollis overheard people talking in Spanish, Greek, Russian, Vietnamese. As the neighborhood became more and more residential it got darker outside: more and more trees, and fewer streetlights. By the time he got to the stop in front of his building it was after six.

Hollis stepped down. The bell rang, and the green-and-white train moved away up the hill. In the lobby of his building, dead leaves that had blown in through the front door lay strewn all over the floor. He took the elevator up to his apartment.

Standing at the window, with his coat still on, Hollis looked down at the darkness of the empty courtyard. He could hear geese honking as they flew by overhead, out of his line of sight. The broken storm window that Peters had dropped lay on a cement walkway, in the middle of a spray of broken glass. The aluminum frame had come apart at one of the corners.

He turned away and lay face down on the bed.

CAPTAIN PICARD

Mr. Data, are you all right?

DATA

I believe I am experiencing some difficulty with my positronic circuitry, Captain. I do not seem to be functioning at full capacity.

PICARD

Can you identify the problem?

DATA

It seems to be some kind of subspace interference, sir. Possibly of alien origin. At the present rate of decay, I estimate the time to total neural net failure at one minute twenty-seven seconds.

Picard stands up and signals the helm.

> PICARD

Ensign, take us out of here: warp nine point five. Dr. Crusher?

> DR. CRUSHER

I'd better get him to sick bay, Captain.

> PICARD

Agreed.

Dr. Crusher bends over Data, who is now lying prone on the bridge. She places her hand gently on his forehead, scanning him with a medical tricorder, then presses her communicator badge.

> CRUSHER

Crusher to transporter room—two to beam directly to sick bay.

> TRANSPORTER ROOM

Acknowledged, Doctor. Whenever you're ready.

She puts her hand on Data's shoulder.

> COUNSELOR TROI

Oh Data, I hope you'll be all right!

> PICARD

And . . . engage!

In the forward viewscreen, stars blur into lines. The *Enterprise* accelerates up to warp speed.

Transporter room: Energize.

Light flares.

They vanish.

FRIDAY, 9:15 P.M.

"Where are you going?" said Hollis. "We aren't getting Blake, are we?"

"I'm trying the other way. By Harvard Street."

Peters tried to pass the slow, rusted-out station wagon in front of them, but a car coming the other way boxed him out.

"The force is strong with this one," he said.

The sky had cleared, and the cold was waking Hollis up. He rubbed his eyes and looked out the window at the shuttered and burned-out storefronts of Brighton scrolling past them.

"What did you do today?" he said.

"Went in to the office. Did some work. Delahay's trying to write this piece about interstellar ether — this stuff they thought was supposed to propagate light through space, or something, before they eventually figured out it didn't exist. In the nineteenth century. The Michelson-Morley experiments. She talks about it all the time now."

"I don't get it," said Hollis. "What do you mean, it propagates light through space?"

A motley crowd of people waited in line outside a nightclub, some sitting, some standing, some milling around talking, not in any particular order. A tour bus parked out front had an air-brushed mural of a barbarian warrioress on it, riding a giant iguana-like lizard. Her bare breasts, impossibly huge and firm, stood out against an idyllic shell-pink sunset.

"Well, they used to think light was like sound. Like, you can't hear anything in a vacuum, because there's no air to propagate the sound."

"But there's still light in a vacuum," said Hollis. "I mean, you can still see, even if there's no air."

"That's exactly the problem, dude, that's why you need the ether to be there to propagate the light. In a vacuum, there's nothing else to do it. Except it turns out you don't have any ether there, either."

"Ah. Now I get it."

Hollis found a loose thread on the front of his coat and snapped it off.

"Fabu."

They turned onto a shabby, patched-up old expressway, criss-crossed with skid marks, and then onto an on-ramp to the Mass Pike. Hollis and Peters watched the traffic for the first few miles without saying anything. They were moving in a fast, tight-packed formation of cars, with nobody slowing down or changing lanes. People were leaving the city for the suburbs and the Cape.

Outside Boston the highway was lit up by a series of yellowish-pink streetlights, and the shoulders on both sides rose up higher and higher the farther from the city they got. By the time they hit the suburbs Hollis and Peters were driving through a kind of artificial concrete canyon, carved out of the landscape of otherwise peaceful neighborhoods. Looking up, Hollis could see dark trees and lighted windows flying past them over their heads.

Ten minutes later they took a curving off-ramp over to Route 128.

"Did you sleep enough?" said Peters.

"I guess so."

"So what did *you* do today? Anything?"

Hollis smiled wanly.

"If I told you, you wouldn't believe me."

An old red pickup truck floated across their lane, from right to left. They watched it cross back again farther ahead and accelerate away through traffic.

"I wonder what it's like to be a weaver?" said Peters. "Who would actually do that? I can remember when my dad was teaching me how to drive, and him saying, 'You see that, son? *That's a weaver.*'"

He held up his index finger.

"And I've never forgotten his words."

"Why don't you try it?" said Hollis.

"What do you mean? You want me to weave?"

"Sure. Look, you can get in right there. Come on, dude, live a little. I'll pay for the ticket. Go for it."

"Oh, come on," said Peters. "What's the point? There's no room, anyway."

He didn't move.

"Besides," he said, "how would you pay for it? With what money? It's not worth it. And since when are you so full of piss and vinegar, anyway?"

"Beats me."

"Anyway, there's some kind of weird police action going on tonight. The streets are crawling with them. When I was driving over to get you there were cruisers everywhere, pulling people over. And vans. People with flashlights, looking in people's cars. I don't know why. State police, highway patrol. Hey, remember what I was saying before, about police? The future is now!"

He pointed at Hollis.

"Oh, I called Ashley: it's no go. I got her machine."

"Whatever," said Hollis. "It's probably just as well."

He was looking out the window. Every minute or so the plain white reflector of a mile marker lit up in the headlights.

"I remember her," he said. "Ashley. Quite the fiery little zippie she was. She must wear colored contacts — nobody's eyes are really that shade of green."

Eyes are nice.

"You're more her type than I am anyway," said Peters.

"I wasn't really on that night."

"Come on, you were a hit. You were a cheeky little R2D2 to my obsequious, servile C3P0."

Hollis could feel the cold through the car window against his right hand. He secretly slipped it up under his shirt and pressed it against his ribs with his other arm to warm it up.

There'll be no escape for the Princess this time.

As time went by the numbers on the exit signs decreased, and Hollis started to feel more alert. Peters turned the radio on and off. They experimented with the moon roof, but it was too cold outside to keep it open. Factories appeared off to one side, with their brand names lit up by spotlights: Polaroid, Raytheon, Mi-

crosoft, BayBank, IBM. When they got to the Dover exit they
swung smoothly off the highway and plunged into the darkness
of the woods. The noise of the traffic and the red and white
streams of headlights and taillights dwindled behind them
through the trees.

They pulled up to the light at the crossroads. Everything was
quiet. Even the throb of the engine was barely audible.

"It's red, Jim," said Peters soberly.

Another car came up behind them, lighting up the interior of
the Lexus with its headlights.

"Once," Peters said, "when I was in high school, I got a pimple on the back of my neck. It was huge — literally, it was the size
of an egg. Wherever I went, whatever I was doing, I was conscious of it. I could feel it, just riding around back there. It was
so big I started to think I could pop it just by leaning my head
back and looking up at the ceiling. I spent a whole day sort of
tossing my head back, over and over again, trying to pop this
God damn pimple on the back of my neck. But I never could.
After a while my neck started to hurt, and I went to the nurse.
She said I had whiplash."

Hollis watched the traffic light, waiting for it to change.

I am now the last human being left alive on earth.

The light changed. The rear wheels sprayed gravel.

This time there were a few stores open in the quiet little sub-
urban strip in the center of town. From the car Hollis could see
two teenage girls in white T-shirts cleaning up behind the
counter at a Steve's Ice Cream, looking very busy and efficient in
the warm, yellow electric light. Past the main commercial area
it got quiet again. The pale fans of sprinklers waved silently back

and forth in the dark, on the front lawns of old Unitarian churches with box steeples.

The roads were narrow and winding, but Peters knew them by heart, and he took them at full speed. Hedges, stone walls, and tree branches flew by, ridiculously close to Hollis's window, and he flinched back a couple of times. For a while Hollis tried to keep track of where they were, but soon he gave up and just relaxed.

At first when they pulled over he didn't recognize it as the same spot where they'd parked that morning. Peters switched off the headlights.

There was a second of silence.

"Suddenly," he said, "I knew fear."

He took out the key, and they climbed out. The doors chunked shut behind them in perfect unison.

"It's better if we park around the corner," he said. "The neighbors might notice the car."

The stars were surprisingly bright. Crickets chirruped wildly in the trees, and they walked away from the car without saying anything. When they turned the corner there were a few lights on in the Victorian farmhouse across the street, but it was quiet.

I am now the last human being left alive

There were lights on in the Donnellys' house, too. The globe on the lamppost was lit, and the light reflected off the dew on the grass.

"They're probably on a timer," said Peters. "Got the keys? Just kidding."

He dug them out of his pocket, saying:

"*My precious, my precious.*"

They set out across the lawn and circled around to the back of the house, looking over their shoulders a little nervously at the house across the street. They stood on the little wooden landing, and Hollis held the screen door while Peters tried the knob on the inner door. It was locked.

"Welcome to the jungle, baby," Peters said softly, as he slid the key in. "You're gonna die."

The door opened. Peters went in first, and when they were both inside Hollis closed it again behind them.

It was pitch black in the little storeroom. Hollis waited while Peters stumbled around in the clutter on the floor.

"How the hell can you see anything?" he said.

Peters didn't answer.

"Motherfucker," he said after a while, and Hollis heard him rattling the doorknob.

"This one's locked too."

"Wasn't it before?"

"No."

Peters sighed and fumbled around with the doorknob some more.

"Is it the same key?" said Hollis.

He smelled dust in the air, and a moment later he sneezed. As his eyes got used to the darkness he could make out the indistinct shape of Peters's broad back, hunched over the lock.

His ability to see through the comfortable illusions of everyday life set him apart from his fellow man.

He heard Peters scratching around with the key trying to find the keyhole, then a grunt of satisfaction. The door opened onto the darkened kitchen. Peters barged in, with his hands together out in front of him like a pistol.

"Freeze, motherfuckers! I'm all over yo' ass!"

He held still for a few seconds, listening. Nothing happened. He relaxed and waved Hollis inside.

Hollis turned on the light. The Donnellys had cleaned up before they left, and everything was even neater and tidier than it had been before. The drainer was empty. The coffee machine was unplugged.

"You know, I wish that girl had showed up," said Hollis, blinking at the light, as he stepped in over the threshold. "The one we met before. What the hell was her name again? Ellen? Evelyn?"

Peters spun around, arms still out, and covered Hollis with the pistol. He sighted down it at him.

"Eleanor," he said.

"Not that I'm bitter or anything."

"The Baroness has a visitor," said Werner. "Your Grace had asked to be informed."

"Very good."

My voice remained steady, despite the emotion his words roused in me.

"You may go."

As soon as I was alone, I stood up and opened the curtains.

There, in that courtyard, I saw them preparing to depart. She was cloaked and muffled as for a long journey, and as I watched he handed her up into a closed carriage. The dogs were silent. He himself mounted up to the driver's seat, taking control of the horses with enviable skill, and at a word from him they lit out for the front gates at a gallop.

I watched them, transfixed—

"Hey," said Peters. "Wait a second." He dropped the gun pose and froze in place, staring off in the direction of the dining room.

Hollis stopped moving and listened.

"What? I don't hear anything."

"No, no, Jesus, *that*. On the table."

Peters pointed into the dining room: there was an open bag of corn chips lying out on the long dining table.

Together Hollis and Peters crossed the kitchen into the dining room, without saying anything, and stood in front of the table.

"What's the big deal?" said Hollis. "They could've just left it out."

"What, and cleaned up the whole rest of the place except for that? It's like Martha Stewart's decontamination chamber in here. Jesus, I bet it's their kid — I bet their kid's home. Don."

"Is that his name?" said Hollis. "They named their kid Don Donnelly?"

He took a couple of corn chips.

"Isn't he going on the trip with them?"

"I don't really know," said Peters. "He could just be house-sitting."

"Jesus, these things are terrible." Hollis looked down at the bag, chewing. "That's what I thought, look: they're baked, not fried."

"What do you expect? His dad's a doctor. And he's some kind of jock, too, I think — look, let's just listen for a minute, maybe we can pick up something."

They stood still for a minute. The house creaked softly with a gust of wind. Peters went over to the window, stepping softly, and cautiously peered out between the curtains.

Patient wakes up after an operation. All the curtains in his room are closed.

Patient: *Hey Doc, how come all the curtains are closed?*

Doctor: *Well, there's a fire in the building across the street, and I didn't want you to think the operation was a failure.*

Peters turned around and cleared his throat.

"Well, there's a car in the driveway. But it was there before — it doesn't mean anything, necessarily."

He clapped his hands and rubbed them together.

"Why don't we split up?" he said.

"That always works in the movies."

"We'll do it like this: one of us goes back outside and walks around the house. Maybe we can see somebody in the window or something." Peters took off his glasses and inspected the lenses, a little nervously. "The other one can just snoop around in here a little."

"Sharp thinking," said Hollis. "Which one of us does which?"

"We'll flip. Do you have a coin?"

Hollis checked his pockets and came up with a nickel.

"Heads," said Peters.

"Jeez, man. Call it in the air."

Hollis flipped. Peters called it again:

"Heads."

When Hollis snapped his hand down to catch it, he missed and open-hand-slapped the nickel across the room and out the door instead. It flew out into the entrance hall and landed silently somewhere on the carpet.

Peters watched it go. He smiled at Hollis.

"I win, by reason of forfeit," he said. "You're on indoor patrol."

He clapped Hollis on the shoulder.

"Don't try to be a hero, kid."

"Story of my life."

Peters started buttoning up his coat.

"Don's room was on the second floor, back in the day, but who knows where he might be now. Anyway, it's probably nothing."

"Sure." Hollis took another corn chip and munched it with exaggerated casualness. "I'll meet you back down here in — I don't know, five minutes?"

"Roger that," said Peters.

He headed off back through the kitchen and out the door. It closed behind him.

Hollis was alone.

Courage, mon vieux.

The chairs at the table were hard and straight-backed. Someone had already pulled one out, and Hollis sat down, slumping down as far as he could. He listened to the house for another minute, biting the insides of his cheeks.

Somebody tapped on the windowpane, and Hollis started up out of his chair, but it was only Peters. He waved apologetically and disappeared back into the darkness. Hollis sat down again.

A wooden clothespin was lying on the table, the old-fashioned one-piece kind without a wire spring, and he rolled up the bag of chips and clipped it shut. From where he was sitting he could see into the living room; there was a kind of plaster proscenium arch around the doorway, with Ionic columns, and medallions at the corners that were molded into elaborate *faux* Book of Kells knots. The grandfather clock whirred into life in the next room and chimed four notes: it was ten-fifteen. With the heels of his hands over his eyes, Hollis let his head sink backwards against the hard wooden chair: he was so tired it was almost comfortable, and his coat cushioned him a little. He started mentally trying to add up the number of hours he'd slept in the past few days, to see how far behind he was, but he kept getting confused.

He leaned forward and put his head down on the tablecloth.

The kitchen door opened. He sat up with a start: it was Peters.

"I hope you were exploring the house with your astral body," he said.

"Something like that." Hollis shook his head, trying to wake up. "Did you see anything?"

Peters pulled out a chair from the table, turned it around, and sat down on it backwards.

"I don't know," he said. "We may have a bogey, on the third floor. There's a couple of lights on up there."

"Did you see somebody?"

"It was kind of hard to tell. Maybe. These glasses aren't that good—I need to get a new prescription."

"I thought you said the lights were on a timer."

"Well, they still could be," Peters said. He shrugged and put his chin down on the back of the chair. "It could be nothing. Did you hear anything in here?"

"No. Nothing."

They were silent, looking at each other.

"All right," Hollis said. "Whatever." He planted his hands on the table and pushed himself up. "I'll be back down in a couple of minutes."

"That's the spirit," said Peters. He pointed his finger at him.

"Eye of the tiger."

Epatez les bourgeois.

The staircase's carpeting muffled his footsteps. He made his way up stooping over, patting the steps in front of him with his hands. When his head was even with the second floor, he scanned the gallery.

The lights were off. It was empty.

From the top of the stairs he could see most of the way down the two main hallways, which led off in opposite directions.

You are in a small, U-shaped gallery.
There are two corridors leading North and South.
There is a staircase leading down.

Through the window, he looked down onto the broad front lawn
and the white circle of light around the lamppost. His breath
frosted on the glass.

The first hallway was deserted — he walked down it briskly as
far as it went, but everything seemed empty — so he jogged back
to the landing the way he had come. As he walked past the head
of the stairs he looked down to the first floor. He could see Peters
serenely reading a magazine by the light of the small chandelier
in the dining room, with his sneakers propped up on the table.

The library was just the way they'd left it, with the two arm-
chairs still turned in a little towards each other. Farther down the
hall was the study, and the pink bathroom where Peters had hidden before, and the cheap Monet print of the haystacks on the
wall.

When he turned the corner Hollis noticed a little dim light
coming from behind one of the doors. He walked towards it, skim-
ming his hand along the wallpaper; the pattern on it was slightly
embossed, and he followed it with his fingers. He was humming
something over and over again under his breath, though he
couldn't remember where it came from or even what the lyrics
were. He crept up to the door: a low rushing, hissing noise was
coming from inside which he couldn't quite identify. The light
was tinted a little, candy colors — yellowish, greenish, pinkish.

Will this fantastic voyage never end?

He tried to look inside, but the door was only open a crack, and
the angle was bad. He listened, but all he could hear was the

rushing noise. After another minute he pushed the door open a little farther.

It was a billiard room. The pool table was in the middle of the room, precisely centered along both axes. A lamp with a green glass shade hung low over the green felt. The balls were all stowed away underneath, and the table was empty except for a few gouged-out cubes of light-blue chalk. The air in the room smelled like tobacco smoke; Hollis noticed an extinct cigar butt in an ashtray on the edge of the table, and he nudged it fastidiously with his finger.

In one corner was a kitschy diner-style jukebox, with glowing pink and yellow tubes running up the sides with little air bubbles rising up inside them. The tubes filled the room with a faint pastel wash. A record was turning on the turntable; the song was over, but the needle was still down, and the speakers were just playing static. The record was "Jailhouse Rock."

A little dorm fridge next to the jukebox turned out to have a flat bottle of gin tucked away in its freezer, encrusted with ice. It was so cold that the gin was slightly viscous, but Hollis poured out a capful and tossed it back. It burned going down. He put the bottle back.

Peters was waiting for him at the head of the stairs, leaning on the railing, studying a painting.

"Anything?" he said in a stage whisper.

"Nothing worth getting too worked up about," said Hollis. "I found some booze — there's a bar in the pool room."

"Ruh-roh," said Peters, in a Scooby-Doo voice. "Well, maybe it'll speed up your reaction times. What do you think of this painting?"

It was an old-master-style portrait of an English noblewoman, blond and petite, in a blue dress with a high neckline.

"Remind you of anybody?"

Hollis peered at it in the half-darkness. She was sitting by herself on a chair in a drawing room, very erect, with a slightly blank expression on her face.

Downstairs the grandfather clock chimed again.

"Help me out here," said Hollis.

"Oh come on, Hollis, it's *Eileen.* Look at it. It's a dead ringer."

Hollis bent down to look closer and sniffed.

"Give me a break," he said. "Listen, I'm going upstairs. The suspense is fucking killing me."

"I'll be waiting. Stay out of trouble."

He trotted back downstairs, and Hollis waited till he was gone before he went around to the next flight.

He went up the stairs to the third floor in a hurry. This time he didn't bother trying to hide, and he walked through the gallery at the top of the stairs without paying much attention to it. Things didn't look very different from the second floor. He thought about taking off his shoes, to make less noise, but he decided he might need them for a quick exit.

It was a race to the edge of space.

Hollis worried about getting lost in the narrow corridors, but somehow he couldn't quite work up the energy to keep track of them. As he strolled from room to darkened room, he blew into his hands. He noticed a little lump in the lining of his overcoat, and while he walked he wrangled it around until he could get it out: it was a superball. He held it up to the dim light: it turned out to be the transparent kind, with multicolored sparkles floating in it. He chucked it down at the floor as he walked, and it bounced up off one wall and down back at him off the ceiling. He snagged it one-handed, but when he tried it again he missed the catch, and it went off his foot and bobbled away somewhere back down the darkened hallway.

He was examining a set of sepia-tinted baby pictures that looked like they might have been taken in the nineteenth century when a pair of headlights flashed in through the front window and swept across the room. He flattened himself up against the wall, out of the light, as they went by.

They'll never take me alive.

The car went past without stopping.

He sighed shakily and ran his hands through his hair.

I can't work under these conditions.

Hollis started to leave the room, but he stopped on the threshold. Down at the far end of the hall, where it turned a corner, a large wooden cabinet stood against the wall. Its shelves were crammed with an incredible assortment of knicknacks: blown- and colored-glass animals, ornamental beer steins, Indian-looking brass figurines with many arms, polished marble eggs, miniature square copper lanterns with glass windows. A huge ornamental serving dish made out of silver or pewter sat by itself on the top shelf. It had a historical scene molded into it.

Something about this last item caught his eye. Even from where he was Hollis could see a thin band of golden electric light reflected in its surface.

The friendly lights of the village still glowed along the shore.

Hollis stood there looking at it. A phone rang somewhere in the house.

Away team to Enterprise. This is an emergency. Come in, Enterprise.

He walked toward the cabinet until he could see his own reflection in the dish, blurry, elongated, upside-down. The parquet creaked under him, and he winced. A little caption engraved in a waving banner along the bottom identified the scene as the Raid on Harpers Ferry. He peered around the corner and saw a door, painted white. Light filtered out from under it, and along the side where it was open a crack. Hollis's palms were sweating, and he wiped them on his jeans. He had to go to the bathroom.

The phone rang again, and again, and then on and on, while Hollis listened without moving. He was weirdly fascinated. There were two different phones somewhere not very far from him, both ringing. One of them had an actual old-fashioned metal bell in it, and in the silences between the rings he could hear it keep on resonating.

There was a plastic *click*, and somebody picked up.

Hollis was still wearing his overcoat. He felt in the pocket, just in case: the blackjack was still there.

Little health insurance.

A woman's voice answered the phone. It came from behind the door with the light on. She spoke in a neutral tone, nicely modulated but indifferent, like a computer counting down a self-destruct sequence.

"Hello?"

There was silence, and a sound like somebody shifting in a chair. Then the voice said:

"Yes, I'll accept."

Hollis walked up to the door. The hinges were on the other side, and he put his hand on the glass knob and pushed it a little farther open. Suddenly he felt afraid for the first time, and everything around him started to take on a slightly jumpy quality, like a piece of cheap animation, or as if he were seeing it by the light of a very fast strobe light.

He leaned forward and put his eye up to the opening.

"Don't move," he whispered, soundlessly. "Don't you move, motherfucker, or I'll blow your motherfucking head off."

His eyes had adjusted to the darkness, and now the light was painfully bright. Even squinting he could hardly make out the room in front of him: there were red carpets, some high bookshelves, a massive wooden desk. It looked like an office, or somebody's study. A dark-haired woman was sitting at the desk with her back to him, in a plush black leather office chair, talking on the phone.

As he crouched there looking at her, she reached over and with a little high-pitched grunt of effort pushed open one of the windows a crack. Immediately the air pressure changed, and a gust of warm air blew down the hall from behind him, lifting some of the papers lightly off the desk and scattering them on the floor. Before he even noticed what was happening, it blew the door in front of him wide open.

The woman swiveled around in the chair.

I'm trying to think who that girl reminds me of. Somebody famous.

It was Xanthe.

She didn't look surprised. She met his eyes with her own large, dark eyes, and with her free hand she covered the mouthpiece of the phone.

Hollis didn't move. For some reason, he didn't know why, his eyes filled with tears.

"Just a second," she said evenly. "It's a long-distance call."

She turned away from him, and he watched her for a second, looking at the back of her head above the padded leather chair, her stockinged foot pointing its toes. Then he walked across the room towards her, slowly, like a sleepwalker. As gently as he could, he took the phone out of her hands and laid it aside on the desk. She didn't resist him. He bent down and gathered her hands together in both of his hands. Then he closed his eyes and kissed her, very, very lightly, on the forehead.

STARDATE 45652.1

 At three in the morning Peters came upstairs wearing a chenille bathrobe with a Park Plaza monogram on one of the pockets. His face was pink, and his hair was wet and slightly wavier than usual. He had a white towel around his neck.

Hollis was in the library, and Peters knocked, softly, before he came in.

"There's like a whole gym in the basement," he said, opening the door. "Check it out — now's your chance to get in some extra reps."

Hollis didn't look up from the magazine he was reading.

"You're such a tourist," he said.

Peters dropped into the armchair facing him and

unwound the towel from around his neck. He shook it out with a flourish and draped it gracefully over his face.

"Ate it," he said.

His voice was muffled by the towel. He burped.

"Drank it. Watched it. Played with it. Bathed in it."

The lights were all out, and Hollis had lit candles. They stood all along the long rectangular room, on different shelves and niches, dripping wax onto ashtrays and sheets of blank stationery. The flames reflected off mirrors and windows and in the glass panels of cabinets and the polished wood of the bookshelves. Hollis cupped a huge glass brandy snifter a third full of red wine in both hands. An open bottle stood on the floor next to him, and there was an empty one lying on its side on the rug, along with an empty six-pack of Corona and a third of a ravaged-looking lime.

"Try some," he said, holding his glass up to the light. "It's expensive — they left the price tag on it."

"I'd rather have some whiskey — I think there's some in the bar downstairs. I hope you didn't drink all that yourself?"

Hollis gave a half-snort, half-laugh.

"Xanthe took care of most of it. She's somewhere upstairs, sleeping it off in one of the guest bedrooms."

Peters pulled the towel off his face.

"I must say, her showing up here was kind of a surprise, in this quarter. Why the hell didn't you tell me about her?"

"Jesus, do you think I knew she'd be here? Before tonight I had no idea if I'd ever even see her again."

"Mmm." Peters mused silently, joggling his knee up and down. "So what's going on with you guys, anyway?"

Hollis sipped his wine again before he answered, staring down into the depths of the glass.

"What's ever going on with anybody?" he said. "She has to get back to the city in the morning, early. She's working."

"How'd she get out here in the first place?"

"I think she has a car."

"You guys should go on a talk show: 'Women who swim with sharks, and the men who love them.' " Peters looked around the library. "You know, it looks like that Sting video in here — what's it called? With all the candles. 'Wrapped Around My Finger.' "

"That wasn't Sting, dude," said Hollis. "That was the Police. They were still together then."

"Oh, listen, I totally forgot to tell you. Guess where Basil's going? Atlanta. We were talking in the car on the way home last night, and he told me all about it. He's getting out of Beantown for good. He thinks Atlanta's the next big scene."

"Why does he think that?"

"I don't know. He didn't say. He probably saw it on *Entertainment Tonight* or something."

"I hope he stays there," said Hollis.

"Oh, he's not that bad."

"He's horrible. I hate that guy."

Hollis looked down at his magazine again.

"Looks like everybody's going somewhere," he went on. "Present company excepted."

Peters levered himself up out of the chair and went over to the window. The blinds were down so the neighbors wouldn't see the lights. He peeked out.

"Coast is clear," he said. "Hey, it's snowing."

"What?"

"Just a little bit. God, what a relief. I thought it would never snow."

"You know, I wish my parents were that rich. As rich as Basil's are."

"Well, they aren't that bad off, are they? Or are they? Do they send you money?"

"They used to." Hollis finished his snifter of wine and set it down on the rug beside his chair. "I think I took it too far, that one time in New York. They had to bail me out of that hotel, you know, and then after that they quit. I guess I ate the goose that laid the golden eggs."

With an effort, Hollis rocked the plump leather armchair back on its hind legs.

"But my, was it scrumptious."

He leaned forward again and poured some wine into a tumbler for Peters, then sat back, dangling his arms limply over the armrests. There was a big TV standing against the wall, hooked up to a Nintendo system. The sound was off, and the screen showed static. Various game cartridges lay scattered around it on the floor. The screen cast a pale gray light over the room, and Hollis stared blankly into it.

"Speaking of which," he said, "I wish there was more food."

"There's like a million more frozen pizzas in that freezer in the pantry. I checked."

"You know Stephen Hawking was our age when he found out he was sick? This is right when it happens to people. And we could turn into schizophrenics, too. Right now. Do you realize that? In your early twenties: that's how long the latency period is, or whatever it's called, before the disease starts showing up. I even knew a guy it happened to. He was in his dorm in college, watching reruns on a black-and-white TV with his roommates. Suddenly he started seeing everything in color. That's how it started. After that he cracked right up."

"What happened to him?"

"I don't really know. It was pretty serious. I think he's in an institution somewhere."

There were some red spots on the rug, and Hollis rubbed his sock over them.

"I hope nobody notices I wined on the carpet."

"Forget it," said Peters. "You can hardly see it."

"He has a tattoo, here"—she touched her neck—*"that will regis-ter only with your augmented vision."*

Peters cleared his throat.

"I meant to tell you," he said. "I saw Eileen the other day. It was just by chance — I met her on the street."

"Oh, yeah? When was that?"

"I don't know. A few days ago. I meant to tell you when it hap-pened. She wasn't with anybody."

"It doesn't matter."

Hollis stared at the candles. The flames made green blobs on his vision, which then stayed in the center of his field of view after he looked away. One of the nearby candles burned un-evenly, a reservoir of hot wax forming around the base. Hollis reached over and pressed his fingertips into it.

"She wasn't a virgin before I slept with her," he said. "I know I told you she was. There were plenty of guys before me."

"Jesus, Hollis. My God, I can't believe you even bothered to lie about that. Nobody cares, dude. Anyway, I never believed you — nobody's a fucking virgin."

"I know."

Peters pushed his hair back behind his ears with both hands.

"Forget about it. Let's do something. Fire up that Nintendo, and I'll whup your ass at something."

"You already whupped it," said Hollis.

"I'll spot you an extra dude."

Peters threw a pillow at his chest. It bounced off him and spilled some more wine.

"Leave me alone," he said. "You're like a fucking camp coun-selor."

The library smelled like melted wax. Peters sighed and stretched out, leaning his head back in the corner of the arm-chair. His pale white legs stuck out onto the rug between them.

Hollis found a pizza crust and chewed on it for a minute, staring at nothing, then got up and got another chair for them to put their feet up on. He restarted the CD and went back to his magazine.

"Look how fat Sally Struthers is now," he said after a while. "No wonder those kids are starving — she ate all the food."

He held up the ad.

"I'm thinking about getting drunk."

"Me too," said Peters. "There's still that bourbon downstairs. Are you buzzed yet?"

"I can't tell," said Hollis. "It's touch and go. I think I'm halfway there."

"I better take out my contacts soon. Oh, guess what I found? In the other room they have one of those Sharper Image automassage chairs."

"Maybe we could just kill them and assume their identities."

They both watched one of the candles flickering and strobing as it went out.

His resources of indifference were immense, his capacity for remorse minimal.

"Let's wake up Xanthe," said Peters. "Consult the feminine perspective."

"Oh, let her sleep. She needs her rest. She's going to be hung over as it is."

"What's this? Does chivalry yet live?"

Hollis sniffed.

"If you can call it living."

He was looking around for the remote control.

"What's her last name, anyway? Xanthe's?"

"Oh, leave it alone, Peters. People like Xanthe don't have last names. Anyway, you're going to jinx us."

Hollis toggled the TV back to a regular channel. It was showing some obscure class of auto racing involving cars that looked like turbocharged station wagons. Once in a while the point of view would switch to a special camera that showed the inside of one of the cars' rear wheels, and every time the car braked its brake pads would glow bright orange from the heat.

"I went by where Eileen's office is today," Hollis said. "That investment company where she works, downtown. That's what I didn't tell you before."

Peters opened his eyes and looked at Hollis.

"What happened?"

"I shouldn't have gone. It was depressing. Brian was there."

"Brian? Jesus. It sounds pretty intense."

"No. Not really. It wasn't at all." Hollis toggled the TV back to static, then shut it off. "It was the opposite of intense, whatever that is."

"I don't know. Boring."

"It definitely wasn't boring."

The grandfather clock downstairs chimed a quarter past three. Hollis reached out with his foot and pressed the fire button on a Nintendo controller lying next to his chair. Nothing happened. There was a hole in his sock, and his pink big toe stuck out.

"What are you thinking about, Hollis?" the young woman asked.

"Someone I once knew. It was a long time ago—"

He shook his head, drawing a hand over his eyes.

"I'm sorry," he said. "It's nothing."

Even for all his melancholy, she found him strangely, almost overpoweringly attractive. It wasn't his fame that drew her to him, or his legendary wealth, or the fabulous mansion in upper Manhattan that he had had brought over, stone by stone, from his estate in Europe. It was something else, something very much deeper, but she couldn't quite put her finger on it—

If only I could do something for him, she thought suddenly. He's so young. So brilliant. So wronged.

She looked up into his piercing eyes.

"Kiss me," she said suddenly, impulsively. "Let me help you forget her!"

"I wonder how fast you'd have to go, if you wanted to stay just on the night side of the earth," Hollis said. "I mean, if you wanted it to be night all the time, forever, and you just kept on moving."

Peters thought for a minute.

"Why don't you just go to Scandinavia?"

"Maybe I will," he said. "Do you remember in grade school, when there was that solar eclipse? We all went outside, and then when it actually happened you weren't even supposed to look at it? I guess it's bad for your eyes, or something — instead we used those cardboard pinhole-projector things, that didn't really work all that well. To tell you the truth, I've always been mad at myself that I didn't just look right at it."

Assuming that the earth is a sphere, if Hollis's present latitude is 42 degrees 20 minutes north of the equator, he would need to match the speed of the earth's rotation along a circle

$$2\pi \ [\cos in \ 42°20' \ (3{,}950 \ miles, the \ radius \ of \ the \ earth)]$$

or 18,347 miles in circumference to remain stationary with respect to a point on the earth's surface.

Given that the earth makes a full rotation approximately once every twenty-four hours, if Hollis were able to move west at

$$\frac{18{,}347 \ miles}{24 \ hours}$$

or just 764.5 miles/hour—slightly faster than Mach 1 at sea level—
he could stay on the night side of the earth forever.

"At least it stays dark longer, now that it's almost winter. I can sleep fine when it's light out, but it's so much easier when it's dark. I never watch the sunrise — I don't even know which way east is, for that matter. When the sky starts getting light I just get so fucking *depressed*. I wonder if there's a name for that. Solar-phobia? Heliophobia? That sickening, baby-blue-colored glow on the horizon. The radiator starts scraping, all the water pipes start banging in the walls. Everybody taking their morning showers. You know, I wish, just once, it wouldn't come up at all.

"And why is it that even though I don't have a job, suddenly I feel like I've just done about a year's worth of work? Answer me that one, laddie. If you can."

Hollis pulled his shabby jacket tighter around him.

"Who would've thought doing nothing all the time would turn out to be so damn tiring?"

Peters took a metal Band-Aid box out of the pocket of his bathrobe. He slid out a pack of Marlboro Lights and offered Hollis one, silently, but Hollis shook his head. Peters took one himself, picking up a short, fat candle to light it with. Hollis splashed the rest of the wine into his glass. Some of it missed, pooling on the tabletop, then spreading slowly until one edge touched the cardboard pizza box. He laid the bottle on its side on the rug next to the first one.

"Two dead soldiers," said Peters, giving it a little kick with his foot.

A minute went by. The smoke from Peters's cigarette floated up in the light of the candles and disappeared into the darkness.

"Did you hear about that guy who used to live in our dorm, in college?" said Hollis, after a while. "I forget his name — he was in the math department. *He* used to stay up all night all the time, practically every night. It was pretty extreme — he would go to bed at like nine in the morning and get up at six at night.

One night Tonga stayed awake until his parents were asleep. Then he slipped out the window and ran down to the docks, where the fishing boats were kept.

"After a while he couldn't stop — he could only get up at night and only fall asleep during the day. It was as if he got stuck. It was weird — he had to go to the hospital. In the end it turned out there was actually something physically wrong with him, like his circadian rhythms were reversed or something, and they had to shine these giant sunlamps on him for a couple of weeks to try to get him back on schedule. He had to take some time off from school."

Ancient legends tell of a time when a flaming disk traveled across the sky in a great arc. Its brightness was such that the whole of the heavenly firmament was rendered a pale blue, and those who gazed on it for more than a moment were struck blind by its brilliance.

Hollis took a sip from his glass. Peters reached over and felt around on the table for the box of Oreos.

I had this dream where we were all on the Enterprise, *from* Star Trek.

Tonga's palms were stinging where the rope had cut them. He turned the other way and looked back out to sea.

"So what happened to him?" said Peters. "The guy who couldn't wake up? Did he ever come back?"

"I don't really know," said Hollis. "It's not like he was a real pal of mine, or anything."

He shrugged and leaned his armchair back on its hind legs again. They creaked ominously.

The candles were all going out. The far end of the room was already almost dark.

"I guess he probably got better."